Puffin Books

SEAWARD

When personal tragedy strikes two young people living thousands of miles apart, they are hurled into an astonishing and dangerous world, a world beyond the realities of everyday life.

Inhabited by fantastical creatures, this hostile yet enchanting land is governed by the malevolent Taranis, who exerts all her magical powers in a bid to keep Cally and Westerly imprisoned in her country. But they must journey towards the sea to reach the destination which will resolve the mystery behind the fate of their loved ones.

With the help of Lugan and his followers, Cally and Westerly embark on a terrifying voyage, facing challenges which draw them together, testing their courage and strength.

Seaward is a remarkable work of magic and adventure, which constantly surprises and sustains suspense right up to the last page.

A master of the fantasy novel, Susan Cooper has written nine books for children, various plays for television and theatre, and four books for adults. She is perhaps best known for the five novels making up the prize-winning *The Dark is Rising* sequence.

Susan Cooper was born in 1935 and gained a degree in English at Oxford, where she was the first woman editor of the university magazine. She joined the *Sunday Times* as a reporter and later became a senior feature writer and deputy news editor. In 1963 she married an American scientist and now lives in Massachusetts, U.S.A.

vv

Seaward

SUSAN COOPER

Puffin Books

PUFFIN BOOKS

Penguin Books Ltd, 27 Wrights Lane, London w8 5tz (Publishing and Editorial)
and Harmondsworth, Middlesex, England (Distribution and Warehouse)
Viking Penguin Inc., 40 West 23rd Street, New York, New York 10010, USA
Penguin Books Australia Ltd, Ringwood, Victoria, Australia
Penguin Books Canada Ltd, 2801 John Street, Markham, Ontario, Canada l3r 1b4
Penguin Books (NZ) Ltd, 183–190 Wairau Road, Auckland 10, New Zealand

First published by The Bodley Head Ltd 1983
Published in Puffin Books 1985
Reprinted 1987, 1988

Made and printed in Great Britain by
Richard Clay Ltd, Bungay, Suffolk
Filmset in Monophoto Photina

For Hume

Chapter I

Westerly came down the path at a long lope, sliding over
the short moorland grass. His pack thumped against his
back with each stride. A lark flicked suddenly into the air a
yard away from him; flew low for a few feet; dropped; flew
again.

'Go home,' he said. 'It's not you they want.'

He strode on without pausing, without turning to see the
bird wheel and dart her watchful way back to the nest. He
had promised himself not to look behind him – not more
than once every mile. He had turned too often in the last
few days, expecting always to see the figures prickling the
horizon, far-off but implacable, following. But each time the
hills had been empty.

Beyond the hollow in the moors that he was crossing
now, the land rose again in a long bony sweep, purple and
green, dappled by cloud shadow. But trees clustered in the
hollow, and faintly he could hear water splashing. He was
thirsty, and hungry too; he had been walking since first
light, and the sun was hot now, halfway up the sky. He
came to a fork in the faintly-marked path, the way trodden
no longer by men but written on the land by the memory of
them, and he turned downhill to the sound of the running
stream.

It ran fast, wider than he had expected, eddying bright
round glistening grey stones. Westerly curled himself awkwardly round a young alder clump and lay flat, splashing
his hot face, drinking until he gasped. Water ran down his
chest as he sat up, making tiny letters out of the tentative

7

dark hair that was beginning to thicken there, and his wet shirt came clammy-cold against his skin.

For a while he prowled the banks of the stream, pausing wherever a rock turned the quick water aside into a pool. Each time he lay flat beside the pool, motionless, staring down; then patiently rose again, shouldered his creased leather pack and moved on to the next. By the time he had found what he was looking for, his shirt was long dry and the sun was high overhead, hot on his back.

He went back through the trees to stare out over the hazy purple moorland, but in all the rolling miles nothing moved.

Westerly lay down again on the bank of the stream, his chin propped on a big overhanging rock, and carefully lowered his right hand into a pool fringed with green weed. His fingers moved, unceasingly but almost imperceptibly, rippling as the weed rippled. Very soon in the cold mountain water his whole hand was numb, but gently he kept the fingers waving, waving, and his arm moving slowly, very slowly, to one side – until with a swift sure lunge he thrust two fingers into the gills of the trout that had hung there all this time resting in the little slow-eddying pool, and he rolled over stiff-armed and brought the fish out twisting silver and frantic on to the grass.

'Sorry,' Westerly said to the flailing bright body, and he hit it once with a stone and it lay still. For a few minutes he sat hunched in the sunshine, turning and twisting his stiff neck, with his cold right hand cradled in his left armpit to thaw. Then he took kindling and a long knife from his pack, made a fire, gutted the fish and held it skewered on the knife to cook. In the sunlight the fire was scarcely visible, after its beginning smoke; only its heat rippled the air. The silver fish blackened and sputtered, and the smell of it made Westerly's stomach clutch at him with emptiness. But before he ate, he went once more to the edge of the trees, to look back.

8

The moors were empty still. Only cloud-shadows moved.

He picked the fish clean and stamped out the dying fire. Then he took the glistening white skeleton, tipped still with head and tail-fin, and laid it across the blackened twigs pointing back the way that he had come. He took out his knife and raised it high, stabbing the blade down into the ground behind the white bone-arrow's tail, and hesitantly, trying to remember, he said some words under his breath.

And the skeleton of the fish called out, in a thin high scream shrilling like a cicada, and Westerly knew that there was danger, that he must go on.

He threw bone and ashes into the swift water, wiped his knife clean, shouldered his pack and set out once more, striding wearily towards the upland path that led away over the hill.

Chapter II

Cally sat in the apple tree It grew less comfortable each year, but it was still her place to be alone. Round her head, leaves dappled the sky, with everywhere among them green bud-small apples clustering. A branch poked into Cally's leg, prickling even through the tough jeans; she shifted, and petals showered round her like spring snow. 'Better keep out of the apple tree,' her father had said that morning, lying frail and listless in bed when she took his breakfast upstairs. 'The blossom will be setting.'

But still she went back. Whenever she climbed the apple tree, she could hear the long soft breathing of the tall poplars that filled the sky beyond the garden; her mother said they sounded like the sea. Cally had never heard the sea, or seen it. She would lie back on a branch sometimes when the wind blew, and try to imagine that she was being rocked by the waves. It was a way of trying to forget the thing she had known for six months now: that her father was dying.

A cowbell clanged from the house: it was her private summons. She slithered down, a twig scratching the back of one hand. When she reached the house a line of tiny red beads of blood had sprung up on the skin; she licked them away tasting salt.

Her mother said, 'Your father's going away for a little while.'

He stood there docile in overcoat and slippers; Cally thought again how small he seemed to have become since he had been ill.

'He's going to a special hospital by the sea,' her mother

said, with a curious mixture of pleading and bravado in her voice. 'The change will do him good.'

Cally saw that the front door was open, and a long dark-blue car standing at the gate. She hugged her father. 'Can we come and see you?'

'Soon,' he said. He patted her shoulder wearily. 'That's my lovely girl.'

Cally's mother pulled up the collar of his coat, and stood with her arm around him. Then there was a tall figure at the front door, reaching down, picking up the suitcase waiting on the floor. Cally stared. It was a woman, older than her mother yet somehow more strongly alive; from the lined pale face and the frame of white hair, startlingly blue eyes looked keenly into her own.

'Hallo, Cally,' the woman said. Her voice was soft, with a lilt of accent.

Cally smiled uncertainly.

'We've met before,' the woman said, 'but only at a distance. We shall meet again soon.' She took Cally's father's arm, very gently. 'We'll take good care of him.'

Cally and her mother followed his slow shuffling way out to the car. A uniformed driver helped him into the back seat, and settled a blanket round his knees; the woman sat beside him. A small sudden wind blew Cally's hair across her face; then the car was gone. She felt a quick surge of fear that she would never see her father again.

Cally's mother took her hand and held it, hard.

'Are you all right?' Cally said.

Her mother said, 'Let's go in out of the wind.' She turned Cally's hand in hers; both were smeared with blood 'You've hurt yourself!'

'Only a scratch,' Cally said. 'And only on the back.

But her mother was looking at the palm as Cally had known she would. The palms of both Cally's hands were strangely marked, and had been since she was born, at the base of the fingers the skin was rough and thickened, so that it was difficult for the hand to curl into a fist. Her mother's hands were the same; it was, she said vaguely, an obscure inherited disease. Cally was used to the ugliness of it, and paid it little attention, but her mother was always concerned that she might damage the thick, slow-healing skin. She said now, anxiously, 'I wish you wouldn't climb trees.'

'Oh *Ma*!' Cally said. She looked up the empty road, after the vanished car. She said, 'I meant to tell Dad – the blossom's all set. There'll be lots of apples this year.'

'The change will do him good,' her mother said.

But she missed Cally's father, and she pined for him. It was a while before Cally noticed the change in her; this was examination time at school, and from morning to night her head was full of Latin verbs and the structures of molecules. Only after the examinations were over did she look properly one day at her mother across the dinner table, and see the shadowed eyes, and the deep lines that seemed not to have been there before. Like her father in his illness, her mother seemed somehow to be shrinking; there was an uncanny look of him in her lean, hollowed face, and a sound of him in her voice, hoarse with fatigue.

Cally said in concern, 'You do look tired. I haven't been helping enough.' She got up to clear the table and looked accusingly at her mother's half-full plate. 'And you aren't eating, Ma.'

Her mother glanced at the plate without interest. 'You always help. You're a good girl. But I am tired – it was all those months when your father . . .' She looked up suddenly, the thin, pointed face like an appealing child's. 'Cally – would you mind if I went to see him, on my own? You can come as soon as school's over. Would you mind?'

'Of course not,' Cally said.

'Your Aunt Tess will come and stay.' Her mother was looking at her but not seeing; she was lost in her own images. 'I may be gone for a while – there are some tests they want to do . . .'

'Tests?' Cally said. 'On you?'

'Just checking up,' her mother said vaguely. 'They want me to go tomorrow. Tess can't come till Sunday, though –'

Cally put an arm round her, feeling suddenly warm and maternal; it was an odd reversal, after all the years of running to her for comfort and support. 'Just don't worry. You go. So long as you can rest while you're there.'

'Oh yes,' her mother said. 'Oh yes. And I shan't be far away.' She patted Cally's hand, and kissed her, but the shadows were still in her face and eyes. Suddenly Cally felt it was a long time since she had seen her mother smile.

But she heard her singing, that night, as she lay in bed: a strange, wordless half-tune that seemed to bring a flicker of memory into Cally's listening head from long ago. Her mother was in her own bedroom; she could hear her moving about.

Cally called, 'Ma? What's that?'

The crooning stopped abruptly. 'Just an old song I used to know.'

'Did you ever sing it to me, when I was little?'

'I may have done. Sleep well, now.'

In a little while she began to hum softly again, so that the music was still drifting through Cally's mind when she fell asleep.

When Cally came home from school the next day, the long dark-blue car was standing at the gate again. The driver jumped out when he saw her, and went round to open the rear door; her mother was sitting inside. She had a blanket wrapped round her knees, just as Cally's father had done, and again Cally thought she looked strangely like him: the same fragility, the same remote, shadowed eyes. She felt fear hollow in the pit of her stomach, but she smiled at her mother and slipped into the car to hug her.

Her mother kissed her cheek gently. 'I've left the telephone number, and everything you and Tess should need. She'll be here the day after tomorrow. Now you're *sure* –'

'I'm going to be fine, Ma. If I get lonely I'll have Jen come over – or I can go to her house. Give my love to Dad. Is he –'

She stopped. After the first talk when they had faced her with the news of the disease that was wasting her father away, her parents had never mentioned it again; it was as if they felt safer in silence.

'There's money in the kitchen drawer if you need it,' her mother said. She kissed her again. 'Don't stay up too late now.'

Cally grinned. 'With Aunt Tess around? Goodbye Ma.'

As she clambered out of the car, a figure in the front seat turned, and Cally saw that it was the woman with silver hair who had come for her father. She said nothing to Cally this time, but only smiled; the blue eyes were bright, watching.

Then the car was moving off, driving down the road. Cally waved it out of sight. She could see the white blur of her mother's face turned, looking back, all the way.

There was an unfamiliar itching in the palms of her hands; she rubbed them absently with her fingers as she went into the house. She was remembering what the silver-haired woman had said when she drove away with her father, that other day *'We shall meet again soon . .'*

In the refrigerator Cally found food for several days, carefully labelled: cold chicken, ham stew to be warmed up ('Heat in double boiler for fifteen minutes,' said the note in her mother's neat hand, 'and DON'T FORGET TO PUT WATER IN POT!') Cally made herself a cup of tea. She

14

had expected to feel lonely but instead was cheerful; to be alone and in charge of the house was like a game, as if she were camping out. She found she was pleased that her aunt would not be coming to keep her company for two days yet.

Then she heard the singing.

It was her mother's wordless humming, the same oddly unfinished tune: a voice in the air. In the first shock she thought it was indeed her mother's voice, that she might have come back for something forgotten, but though she went through every room in the little house, in search of the singing that gently filled it, there was no one there. She checked the radio and television sets, and the record-player: all were firmly switched off. Yet the singing went on, soft, insistent, coming from nowhere: rhythmic waves of melody repeated over and over again. Cally was too puzzled to be alarmed. She sat on the stairs, chin on hands, listening, and gradually the singing died away.

After a while she thought she must have imagined it. She ate some supper, talked to her friend Jen on the telephone, watched a television film and went to bed. She slept deep, but when night faded to day she began dreaming of the apple tree at the end of the garden. She was sitting up there between the embracing branches, swayed by the wind, looking out at the great poplars that sounded like the sea, and the steady rustling breathing of the poplar trees grew higher and louder, filling her ears, wave after wave, filling the air. Cally woke gently out of her dream, the sound carrying her into consciousness as if she were borne in a boat – and when she was awake she found she could hear the singing again.

It was the same voice, the same melody, but not continuous this time. The familiar phrase came twice or three times, then died gradually away into silence. For a few moments she would hear nothing, and then a snatch of it came again, far away. Silence once more: then it was back, clear close, yet still untraceable.

Cally padded into her parents' empty bedroom and picked up the telephone.

'Jen?'

'Cally! I'm not awake. Are you awake? D'you know it's only seven o clock in the morning? On a *Saturday*?'

Sorry ' Cally said.

'Lucky I got to the phone first. If you woke my dad –

'I'm *sorry* ' Cally said. 'I didn't look.

Jen said, more normally. 'What's up?

I can hear that singing again.

Like last night?'

Uh-huh.'

Wow.

'It's just the same, the voice like Ma's. the same song Only now it comes and goes.'

'You sure she isn't there?'

'Of course I am.'

'Hiding under the bed maybe.' said Jen. and giggled.

'Listen!' Cally said suddenly. 'There it is again, much louder. all round me. Listen!' She held the telephone out to the room, to the air filled now with the strong sweet voice. the curving half-shaped melody pulsing in her ears. Then she brought the receiver close again. You hear?'

I can't hear anything.' There was no longer a laugh in Jen's voice. 'Except the wind. Look. Cal, there's half a gale blowing outside. It must be the wind in the chimney. or the telephone wires, or something.'

Cally said, 'It's a voice, singing.'

Around her. the singing faded once more into a thread of sound, far away. that she could scarcely hear.

'That's weird. Cal, that's really weird. You better come stay over here.'

'You ever heard the sea?' Cally said, straining her ears to catch the plaintive rise and fall of the distant song. 'I think it must sound like the sea. A long way off.'

'Come on over.' Jen said nervously. 'Come and eat breakfast. I'll cook sausages.'

'I'll call you back.' Cally said. She put down the receiver and went out on to the landing, listening, hunting the sound. Nothing. She washed, pulled on a shirt and some jeans, went back into her parents' room—and then all at once the singing was back. different. enormously loud. and suddenly Cally was frightened.

The voice was strident, demanding. The phrase that had been a haunting, plaintive lilt in her mother's first gentle crooning had changed now to a pattern of hammer-blows. beating at her ears. Cally wheeled about, her hands up in defence, terrified.

'Ma! Ma!'

It was instinctive, a cry for help. *Where are you? I need you. I don't know what to do. where have you gone? Ma, Dad, I can't do without you, you've always been here, come back, come back . . .*

But they weren't there in the empty house; she was alone with the beating voice. She knew it was not her mother's voice, for sure now: the harshness and fury in it were totally alien to that familiar gentleness. But why was this the same music her mother had sung, that last day?

Cally had a sudden nightmare image of her mother hostile to her. of a malevolence aimed at her which somehow was retribution for everything she had ever failed to do, or done wrong. In place of the loving forgiveness she had always known, in her mind she saw her mother's face twisted with ill-wishing, fierce as the throbbing song which so pressed on her now that she thought her head would split.

She whirled round again in the small sunny room and came up against her own image in a mirror. It was hardly recognizable: the face blurred like the face of a small distraught child, cheeks tear-stained, eyes red and staring. Cally looked at herself in horror. Behind her reflected figure.

17

green branches tossed in the wind, the green of the tall poplar trees filling half the sky outside. She gazed wildly at them, clutching for comfort from the reflection, and saw around them the carved frame of the tall cheval-glass mirror that was her mother's pride and joy, brought from some life before Cally had been born. Fish swam around the mirror, carved in oak, between leaves and strange flowers. She had enjoyed running her fingers over them when she was small; she remembered how she used to creep into the room when her mother was dressing, and how she would slip behind the mirror and tip it gently and her mother would haul her out, laughing . . . *Remember, remember* . . . She put her hands over her ears, fighting the harsh throbbing voice.

The sound grew no less, but rose unbelievably higher, louder: suddenly it seemed terrifyingly close behind her in the empty room. Cally could bear it no longer, she could think of nothing but that she must get away before it drove her mad. Without thought, she thrust her hands out to the mirror, pressing her rough-skinned palms against the cool flat glass.

And the glass seemed to melt under her hands as if it were water, and took her in, and she stepped through the mirror out of the room.

Chapter III

Westerly paused and looked about him; all around, the hills rolled to the horizon, purple and brown and green, curving one upon the other like lines of great sleeping animals. He was on the roof of the high country. Before him the faint grassy path rose higher still, through scrubby heather and gold-starred bushes of gorse, to the line where land met sky.

He forced himself on, feeling his pack heavy on his shoulders. The sun blazed down; he heard the swish of his feet over the grass, and the small song of the wind. Then gradually he thought he began to hear other sounds, bizarre, improbable: distant voices calling, and the clash of metal, and once the muffled neighing of a horse.

He swung round and looked behind him, over the rolling hills, but saw no movement, no one following.

At last he reached the crest, and suddenly facing him in the flaring sunlight was a great sweep of sky, the land falling away steeply at his feet. For a mile or more below him, the moorland lay flat, like a huge plate set into the hills – and the new sounds were loud in his ears, rising from a strange pattern spread down there, bright against the brown land.

He stared, disbelieving. All over the plateau, spread in the shape of an immense square, he saw gleaming clusters of men in blue or gold: swaying, hovering in their places. He saw a crowd of golden foot-soldiers, waving swords, shouting behind the blazing reflections from their shields; among them he saw a group of horsemen in blue robes, blue banners flying. spears held for the charge but the horses held in check. waiting.

He saw towers so like castles that it was a shock to look again and realize that they were mounted on wheels, to be tugged and pushed by other groups of foot-soldiers in blue or gold. In another cluster of horsemen he saw a single mounted figure in black, holding a tall glistening cross high on a pole. Each small crowd seemed full of a fierce energy – and yet none moved. A shout rose from the far corner of the patterned throng, where most of the clustering. figures shimmered sky-blue, and all at once a group of golden horsemen cantered forward through the motionless, menacing figures around them. turned abruptly to one side and reined in, their horses whinnying with impatience.

The movement seemed oddly. bafflingly familiar. Then above his head Westerly heard a voice, soft and musical and yet seeming to fill the whole sky. It said with amusement. Knight to king's pawn four. But that will do you no good at all.'

Westerly looked up. He had thought himself on the crest, but on a slope above him, two figures stood. He could not see them clearly against the bright sky, but they seemed far taller than human height: one a hooded form wrapped in a gleaming golden cloak; the other a woman, blue-robed, her hood flung back to show a mass of waving hair so fair it seemed to be white.

She turned to him, and he could not distinguish her face but knew that the eyes suddenly holding his gaze were a strange bright blue. She looked at him for a long time, and at last she said, 'You should not be here in this country. Westerly.'

He said huskily. 'I came through a door.'

And who showed you how?'

'My mother,' he said. 'Before they – killed her. His voice shook. and he dug his fingernails into his palms.

20

She showed no emotion. She glanced once at the figure in gold, but his back was turned. Then she looked coolly back at Westerly, the blue eyes flickering past him to the hills over which he had come. 'And you think yourself pursued,' she said. 'You are running.'

Westerly said nothing. The strap of his pack was cutting into his neck, but he dared not move.

She turned away from him, back to the frozen blue-gold armies spread on the land below, and raised her arm. 'Bishop to king's pawn four,' she said, and laughed.

Far below, the ordered lines erupted; cutting through in a sudden sweep of speed the figure in black came galloping, cross held high, blue-clad horsemen moving close beside him. They charged full tilt at the golden knights who had moved before, and the knights stood waiting, watching, unmoving. Westerly stared in horrified fascination, tensing for the clash.

But none came. As the blue reached the gold, there was a flicker of light rapid as the blink of an eye, and suddenly the golden knights were not there.

Westerly heard himself gasp.

The woman laughed again, and again he felt her eyes on him. 'Running,' she said. 'But where will you run to?'

It was a question filled with his own fears, making him feel small and lost, and he would not look at it. He turned to look down at the living chessmen on the plain, and he said suddenly, irrelevantly, 'Why aren't they black and white?'

The answering voice was not hers. It came from the other tall figure, hooded in its heavy gold robe: a deep voice, catching oddly at some memory he could not find.

'Nothing is black and white, Westerly, in this long game we play.'

'They are coming, Westerly,' the woman said. She leaned towards him. 'They are coming, and the white bones will not help you. You must run, and the way ahead lies across the plain – and you cannot cross it before they reach this hilltop. They will see you.'

There was no escape from the fear. Westerly looked desperately out at the long sweep of the plateau, stretching far beyond the living chessboard to a distant misted skyline where the hills rose again. 'Yes,' he said miserably. 'They will.'

Her voice softened, gentling him like music. 'We will give you a chance,' she said. 'It is only a chance – you must remember that. But if you choose to gamble, we will give you a chance for freedom by putting you into our game.'

He looked hard at her, but the sun was sinking lower now, shining into his eyes, and still he could not make out her face. And inside the hood of the gold-robed figure beside her, he could see nothing but shadow. He thought wildly: *into our game?*

'All right,' he said.

The gold-robed man stood still as an owl, facing him.

'Remember, you take the chance,' the woman said, clear and loud, with a note of triumph. She laughed. 'Well then – will you be the gold, or the blue?'

Westerly felt a great sense of release, all his tense watchfulness dropping away from him like ropes cut from a prisoner. He was safe; gratitude flooded warm through his mind. But just as he would have given himself to her blue-clad army of followers, the deep voice of the other said with curt authority, 'He will go to the gold.'

She turned, almost petulantly. The voice from inside the hood said, more amiably, 'You are winning, after all.'

'Very well,' she said.

And in an instant Westerly found himself among men and boys dressed in the same glinting gold as the robe of their master, and his ears were full of shout and clatter. The air was warmer. He was down on the plain; the hill rose

22

above him. An arm shoved him, a voice said, 'Hey you – what's y'r name again?'

Westerly said, bemused, 'West – Westerly.'

'Well watch it, West – keep position.'

'Position?'

'Five feet each of us from the other, the man said – you deaf? Have to be, to miss *him*.'

He grinned, a pleasant battered face creasing under the golden cap, and jerked his head at a chunky red-faced man bellowing orders at all around him. Red Face caught sight of Westerly.

'Get back, that man there! *Whatta you think you're doin'?* Havin' a little chinwag, eh? *This ain't no picnic!*'

Westerly moved hastily sideways, and Red Face turned his attention to another disorganized soldier. 'Get in position, get in position! *You're in the army, son . . .*'

Gradually over all the vast field sounds died away, until there was a long hush broken only by the distant whinny of a horse, and the clash of a dropped shield. Down here, Westerly could see nothing of the pattern that had seemed so clear from above; there was only his group of men scattered obediently at their five-foot intervals, and fifty yards away another identical gold-clothed platoon. He could smell sweat, and dung, and the dirt of the field. He realized belatedly that he held a sword in his right hand, and that the other arm and hand were thrust through the leather thongs of a heavy round shield: he felt the weight of the strange golden tunic and trousers he wore

There was no weight on his shoulders. He thought in panic of his pack, and spun round, searching, anxious.

His neighbour hissed, 'Stand still!'

'But I've lost –'

'*Shut up!*'

Red Face was turning. Westerly froze, staring rigidly ahead. The big man looked at him suspiciously, but turned away again. The field was still, prickling with tension. Somewhere far off, a lark's bubbling song rose into the air.

Westerly whispered, 'What are we waiting for?'

'Their next move, of course. Keep watch – all around you. You never know what'll come.'

'And what if it comes?'

'Stand.'

Westerly glanced at him. The weatherbeaten face was grim, the eyes darting nervously round, straining to see any movement on the field.

'Stand?'

Sing-song, the man said, 'Stand. Whatever happens, stand fast.'

'And there's nothing you can do to escape,' Westerly said.

'No.'

'Then what's the point of watching?'

The man frowned, intent, and shook his head impatiently.

Westerly looked up and saw the two tall figures, one gold, one blue, standing high above them on the slope. He said, 'But it's *his* move.'

'What?'

'The players – up there. It's his turn – and we're his men.'

The man glanced up at the slope, and then back at Westerly, frowning. 'You crazy? What players? There's no one up there. There's only this, here. Just wait, and be ready.'

Faintly from the nearest group of golden soldiers a shout rose: '*Charge!*' All together, in neat formation, they ran another fifty yards further from Westerly's troop; pausing then, only dimly visible, in the same stillness as before.

Looking up, Westerly saw the arm of the gold-robed figure raised, pointing at the move it had made; then it dropped. He watched the blue. There was a pause; he could just see

24

the light of the dying sun glinting on the woman's bright hair. Then, slowly, she in turn raised her arm.

In the moment of stillness he tried desperately to re-member the pattern of the living pieces on the great chess-board as he had seen them from above, but he could not find the image. All around him were the grim, dogged faces, waiting, unquestioning. He heard shouts and a huge rum-bling, and towards them over the field one of the moving towers came inexorably bearing down, blue-clad soldiers all around it, heaving, yelling.

Red Face bellowed, 'Stand firm! Stand!'

A rebellious fury flooded Westerly's mind: why should he stand and wait to be destroyed? What was the matter with them all, blindly obeying the whim of someone they couldn't even see?

He ran. He heard the furious voice raised: '*Come back that man!*' Stumbling through the grass and scrub he looked over his shoulder and saw the great blue tower reach his own motionless gold group of soldiers – and saw that suddenly the soldiers were no longer there.

But the rolling, lumbering tower did not pause. Veering round, seeing through huge hidden eyes of its own, it made straight for Westerly; and as if this were a signal, both armies as one turned and charged in its wake. From all sides they came rushing at Westerly: blue-clad horsemen yelling and whooping, golden infantrymen grimly waving their swords. He stared in horror for an instant, all his fear of pursuit re-awakened and roaring in his ears; then flung himself forward, running for his life. He tossed away his sword; tore the shield loose from his arm and threw that too. It bounced clanging on the hard ground, and within a terrifyingly short moment clanged again to tell him a gal-loping pursuing horse had kicked it aside. Gasping for breath, Westerly ran and ran, despair fogging his mind as the tumult of shouts and yells grew louder, nearer, nearer –

Then suddenly behind him there was total silence. He could hear only his own long rasping breaths, and the thudding of his blood in his ears. He glanced back, and astonishment caught his stride and sent him sprawling on the grass. No one was there. Over all the plain no trace remained of that crowded mingling of blue and gold; every horse, every man was gone. Westerly crouched on hands and knees, panting, staring at the empty grass, hearing only the small whine of the wind.

Confused words and images darted through his head.

'They are coming, Westerly,' she had said. 'They will see you.' And it was true; he knew himself pursued. 'We will give you a chance for safety by putting you in our game.' But she had not given him safety, she had given him a still more desperate pursuit; each time he ran from one danger, he ran into one that was worse . . .

Then he understood. *'In our game.'* His running had saved him after all; it had carried him out of her perilous game, over the edge of the chessboard, back into the world. And he was wearing his own clothes now, and the weight of his pack was on his shoulders again.

Stumbling to his feet, he saw a small hawk hanging high in the blue sky.

Ahead, on the far side of the plateau, a dark line of trees marked the beginning of wooded, rising land. The horizon was gold-rimmed where the sun was going down; the light was reddening in the sky. Westerly shivered, as the breeze chilled the sweat on his face. He began to walk, swinging once more into the familiar long-distance lope; travelling.

Chapter IV

The light was almost gone when he reached the edge of the trees. Westerly hesitated. He looked back across the plain; lightning flickered silently over the hills from which he had come, and he could just make out a long mounded line of dark cloud. Turning to the scattered pines edging the forest ahead, he saw a faint glow of light somewhere within the trees. Cautiously he moved towards it, and saw that the light beamed out from the window of a small log house. He hung back in the shadows, watching.

The door of the house opened and a tall figure came out, bending his head to duck under the lintel. He stood there for a moment, a dark silhouette in the bright doorway. Then he moved, so that the light pouring out past him from the house glinted golden over his body, and Westerly saw that it was the chess-player from the hill.

The tall man said softly, to the trees, 'Come in, Westerly. You must travel no more tonight.'

Westerly stood silent for a long time, caught between wonder and doubt, while the man waited patient and unmoving in his golden doorway. At last the weight of his pack made Westerly shift his feet, and a twig cracked loudly. The man's head turned, but he did not move.

Westerly said, clear and deliberate, 'What would have happened to me, if I hadn't run?'

'She offered you a chance, and you took it,' the man said. 'You knew that it was only a chance.' His voice was deep and mild, but every word distinct.

'I'd have been . . . *nothing*. Like them.'

Yes. said the man in gold. 'Very likely. Particularly if you had found yourself in her livery. There are things I must tell you about the Lady Taranis.' He turned in Westerly's direction. holding out his hand. 'Come in. out of the night.'

Darkness had filled the air: Westerly could see nothing around him but the dim outline of the nearest trees. He hated the nights in this land, hated the chill that his blanket could only just keep at bay: the small menacing sounds from every direction, hissing. crackling. breathing: the nervous shallow sleep. the half-sleep of an animal, that was all he could ever allow himself. But still he paused warily watching the man in gold.

The man shifted impatiently. 'Listen, then.' he said. 'I will tell you about yourself. You come from another country. You are Westerly. travelling, and you fear those who perhaps follow you, and would kill you if they caught you. You are searching for your father.'

Westerly stood very still, listening.

'You travel seaward.' said the man in gold. 'because your mother told you that it was the sea which would take you to him. though she did not tell you where, or when, or how.' He paused for a moment, looking round restlessly at the trees. 'The nights are not your friend in this country. boy – you must come in. There are three things of which your mother did tell you. Have you forgotten them?'

Westerly heard in his mind his mother's voice, low and urgent, in the last moment that he had seen her. *'You will meet three that you can trust: a man with eyes like an owl, a girl with selkie hands, and a creature in a high place. Go bravely. I love you.'*

He felt for the knife in his pack, to be sure that it was in easy reach. Then he went forward into the light, up to the doorway. The man in the golden robe stood there unmoving: Westerly looked up at him. He saw a lean, lively face under a tousle of gold-brown hair: the mouth had lines of laughter round it. and the eyes dancing at him were bright and strange. a tawny brown flecked with gold.

The man smiled a little. 'Well?'

'Eyes like an owl.' Westerly said. 'Weird.' He grinned suddenly. and went in through the log-framed door.

The brightness inside made him pause. blinking. It was a single arched room, running the length of the house; lanterns burned on all four walls and on a rough wooden table set in the middle. and flames leapt in a high stone fireplace that filled the far wall.

The man in gold latched the door behind them and swung off his long cloak: he was still a regal figure. in jerkin and trousers as tawny-gold as his eyes.

Westerly said. 'Who are you?'

'I knew your mother once,' the man said.

'In that country or in this?'

'In both.'

'But who are you?'

'Lugan.' said the man. 'You may call me Lugan. And while you are in my house. give no thought to those who may follow you. Sit down.'

He crossed to the fire and took the cover from a black iron pot standing beside it; the smell that rose filled Westerly's mouth with water. and his stomach felt suddenly as if it were flat and empty against his spine. Lugan filled two bowls with a thick aromatic soup heavy as a stew; set them on the table and broke chunks from a loaf of dark crusty bread. 'Eat.' he said. smiling. 'That was a small fish, and it was a long time ago.'

Westerly was too hungry for wonder; they sat opposite one another at the table. and there was no talk for a while. Then he said through a mouthful, 'D'you know *everything* that happens?'

Lugan sat playing with a piece of bread, frowning a little

the youthful lines of his face turned sombre with thought. He said at length, 'I am your . . . watchman. As a hawk hangs watching in the sky, I see those things that happen to you – but only when they are happening, not before. Sometimes I may intervene. Not always. There are perils in this country, but there are also laws – and while you journey here, I watch that neither you nor anyone else break those laws.'

Westerly chewed on a crust. 'You're a sort of policeman.'

The big man snorted with laughter, and shook his head. 'I do what I choose. Did your mother never speak of me?'

Westerly shook his head. 'She taught me –' He hesitated. 'She taught me some things ordinary people don't learn. She was – special. She talked about my father a lot, and she always said that one day I'd go off to look for him. And that the same people who'd taken him away would come after me. She didn't say anything about you – or the lady.'

Lugan stood up abruptly, his head almost brushing the ceiling. 'No. The Lady Taranis is not often spoken of, anywhere.' He sighed. 'Taranis. She is brightness and she is darkness, she is kind and she is cruel. She is – unpredictable. This is her country. And so perhaps is the one from which you came.'

He reached one long arm up to a shelf on the rough log wall, and brought down a wooden box. Westerly looked at it curiously. All its sides and top were intricately carved with the forms of dragons, coiling and interweaving, with tiny red gems set in their scaly heads for eyes. Lugan took a key from his pocket and unlocked the box.

'I cannot keep her from you,' he said. 'She will come whenever she chooses. Sometimes she may help you, sometimes her treachery will engulf you like a wave. The only protection I can give you against the lady is this.'

He lifted the lid of the dragon box and took out a small bundle wrapped in red cloth, the corners knotted together over the top. He held it out. Westerly took it gingerly; it was heavy and oddly-shaped, but no larger than his fist.

Lugan said, 'Do not untie the knots until you need strength. And then take care. She will –'

He broke off suddenly, his head up, listening. He said abruptly, 'Cover your ears.'

But the sound was already filling Westerly's head and mind, the high sweet wordless singing, filling every corner of the room: soft, gentle, yet totally overwhelming. He felt the music all around him as if it were water, as if he were drowning; he could not tell where it came from. He clutched the edge of the table. In a blur he saw Lugan's lean face dark with anger, but he too seemed held powerless by the singing. And then, out of the music, the Lady Taranis was in the room.

Her white hair glinted in the firelight; the blue robe shimmered like a sunlit sea. She stood beside them, looking bright-eyed at the little cloth-wrapped bundle in Westerly's hand.

'Presents,' she said petulantly, looking up at Lugan. 'You never give *me* presents.'

His deep voice was expressionless. 'You have always taken what you wanted.'

Taranis shook her head, smiling. 'I try to,' she said. 'But sometimes I am prevented.' She laughed, and turned her head to Westerly; he gazed fascinated at the brilliant blue of her eyes. 'And here is our chance-taker,' she said, 'who is travelling to the sea, and has the wit not always to do what he is told. I like that, Westerly. You will do well – if they do not catch you first.'

Westerly said, resentment making him bold, 'And if I'm not turned into thin air, like a chessman off a board.'

She laughed again, like a delighted child. 'How could you think I would let that happen?' The warmth in her voice was like an embrace; Westerly could feel it wrapping him

31

round, easing away his wariness. He made himself resist it. Staring at her, he eased his hand down beside his chair to his pack; his fingers quietly slipped the knotted bundle inside, and took firm hold of the carrying strap.

Taranis held his gaze. Her voice came low and coaxing. 'Come with me, Westerly. I will take you to the sea, and there shall be no more pursuing and no more peril. Come with me, and I will send you over the ocean, to the land of the Tir n'An Og, the ever-young, where there is neither loss nor age nor pain. You will find your father there.'

Westerly could feel the tense stillness of Lugan's big figure across the table. He said, 'That may be what I shall find, in the end. But I must go seaward on my own.'

Taranis said softly, 'Oho.' She flicked a glance at Lugan, the blue eyes suddenly cold; then smiled again at Westerly. There was an edge to the voice now. 'I could take you, if I chose. Because I like your looks. Oh yes, I could take you '

Lugan's deep voice said quietly, 'I think not.'

She swung round to him, glaring. 'We shall see.'

Before Westerly could take a breath, she moved one swift step backwards, a whirl of blue and white, and she raised one arm and pointed. And from every stub and knot-hole in the logs that were the walls, all at once branches were growing, twining, reaching out; green leaves brushed their faces, and sprays of blossom fragrant as spring. The house was a woodland suddenly; there were no more walls, but a gentle jungle of leaves and bloom and scented air. Westerly's fingers clenched hard round the strap that they held; it was the one firm point in a world of dream. He could no longer see Lugan through the leafy branches.

But he could see the Lady Taranis. She was younger now, many years younger, the blue eyes glowing in a smooth sweet face no older than his own. Her white-blonde hair was a cloud of curls like the tendrils of the honeysuckle twining over his shoulders, and she wore flowers in her hair. She laughed at him, and reached out her hands, white and young and beckoning. She belonged to the leaves and the blossom and the greenwood, and she was calling him there, to fleet the time carelessly, as they did in the golden world . . .

He ached suddenly with the burden of loneliness that he carried always now; he yearned for brightness and laughter and the spring. And perhaps he would have reached out his hand to hers and gone with her – but there was all at once a hissing through the rustle of the wind in the leaves, and a dark look of rage and alarm twisted Taranis' young face. And through the lovely wilderness around them came twining and twisting the scaly spined bodies of dragons, golden and green and brown. Like great armoured eels they crashed through the graceful trees, their spiny folded wings ripping the leaves, their long teeth agape and gleaming. Their red eyes shone like live coals fanned by the wind. Westerly leapt backwards, clutching his pack like a shield, and a strong hand took him by the shoulder.

Lugan was towering over him, his craggy face stern. In his other hand he held the carved wooden box, and from its writhing sides the dragons were leaping out, growing monstrously as they came, hissing and crackling like fires. His deep voice came low and urgent.

'Go, boy – go westerly, as you are named. Go your own way to the sea, in what company you choose. Follow the sun. I shall watch for you.'

A high terrible shriek rose from the tumult around them.

'But Taranis –'

'Go!'

He swung Westerly about, and sent him stumbling through the trees.

And in a whirling moment all the turbulent noise was gone. There were no enveloping fragrant blossoms, no seething dragons; there was no Taranis, no Lugan. There was only a silent woodland of towering wide-set beech trees, their grey trunks reaching high to a green canopy overhead. and the only sound was the rustle of Westerly's feet treading the brown carpet of dead fallen leaves.

He walked blindly on through the wood, in the sunlight filtering down through the roof of branches, and he began to hear the music of water running. He came to a stream tumbling through the trees, and he followed it to a place of slower. deeper music. where abruptly the woodland ended and the stream lost itself in the broad waters of a river.

Westerly stood on a rocky bluff, looking out. The river was wide and smooth as a giant highway; moving slowly. but ruffled by rapids in the distance where it turned a bend. Thickets of alder and poplar lined the far bank, with the beech trees rising again behind them Looking directly down at the water from the high bank on which he stood, he saw a small boat moored below.

He scrambled down. It was a battered wooden dinghy with two thwarts: old, but dry inside. Two oars lay in the bottom, and a small anchor with a coil of line. The boat was tied up to an iron post set firmly into the bank; it lay there rocking gently, pulled backwards by the tug of the current.

Westerly hesitated for a moment. held by memories of all the hours he had spent helping boatmen on the broad river near his home. Then he threw his backpack into the boat and climbed in after it. Lying in the centre of the coil of anchor line he found three brass rowlocks. He picked them up, feeling the warmth of the sun in the metal, and looked for the holes set for them: two in the sides of the boat, one in the stern. The boat was an exact copy of those he had always known. He fitted in the stern rowlock, and pulled out one oar to be ready for it. Then he looked at the bow line tied to the post, and hesitated again. Even in this country, he had scruples about taking a stranger's boat. uninvited. 'There are laws,' Lugan had said.

34

But they were not the laws of policemen.

The dinghy rocked as Westerly moved, and below one thwart a bright point of light caught his eye. Crouching, he reached down. The light blinked red. He picked up a piece of wood half the length of his hand, hard to see against the wooden bottom of the boat. It was carved in the shape of a dragon, and set with two tiny red gems for eyes.

Westerly looked at the dragon: at the delicately carved scales and the small sharp teeth. Then he slipped it into his pack, and with a new confidence cast off the boat from the iron post. Its bow swung slowly round in the current. Westerly set the oar in the stern rowlock and stood there to scull. With a tug, the water caught the dinghy and carried it out into midstream, travelling with the river travelling wherever the river might go.

In the blue sky overhead, a small hawk hung in the air, looking down, watching.

Chapter V

Cally stepped through the mirror, out of the room, and the world blurred as if she were swimming underwater. Then her eyes cleared and she was walking, walking down a broad path with tall, straight-trunked pine trees towering dark on either side. She looked back. Nothing was there but the pine trees. A soft layer of needles covered the path, and her footsteps made no sound. At the edge of the trees, ferns grew green in a thick fringe. Far overhead, where the pines reached together in a high arch, she could hear the wind in the treetops, breathing.

Cally walked slowly, automatically. She felt dazed, detached, as if she were living a dream. *Where am I? How did I get here? Where am I going?* Half-formed, half-heard, the questions floated aimlessly at the back of her mind.

The path seemed to have no end. Before her and behind, it stretched on and on, dwindling into the darkness of the trees. Sometimes as she walked she thought she could hear a distant thudding like the chopping of wood, but whenever she paused to listen, it died away. Then ahead, at the edge of the trees, she saw a signpost.

It stood beside the path among the tall feathery ferns, pointing into the forest. Its post was green with lichen, and Cally could see no word written on its blank pointing arm. In the direction of its pointing, there was no trace of a trail cut through the woods. There was nothing but the trees. The signpost pointed nowhere.

Yet it gave her a direction; it was better than the endless straight shadowed path. She plunged through the ferns and into the trees, following the signpost's blind finger.

Almost at once she was lost. The ground was rough and treacherous, hummocked with moss-covered boulders and rotting branches that caught at her feet. Stumbling through the trees, ducking beneath dead trunks that leaned against the living, Cally turned this way and that, fighting her way through low leafless twigs with her hands up to shield her face. Overhead a squirrel chattered shrilly at her, but she could not see it. Sometimes she found herself clambering over small rocks piled in long broken heaps, as if they were the fallen remnants of what had long ago been walls. But the wood had swallowed the walls, grown over and through them.

She thought again that she heard the thudding of an axe somewhere far off, but could not tell it from the rhythm of the blood beating in her ears.

The pines were thinning out now; they were smaller, with ferns and scrubby undergrowth between them, and Cally could see broken cloud in the sky above. Then, looking ahead, she saw something among the trees that was not a tree: a dark, straight pillar half as tall again as a man. She went towards it; then caught her breath and stood still.

It was a pillar of granite; its white-flecked surface gleamed dully in the grey light. But it had a head. Carved into the top of the pillar, so lifelike that it seemed about to move, was the face of a woman. The features were clear and beautiful, framed by long waving hair that flowed down and into the rough-cut stone beneath; the mouth smiled, and the eyes were welcoming. There was a gentle kindliness in the face that made Cally feel warm, cherished, as if the sun shone. She looked at it for a long time, feeling her taut wariness gradually relax – until she moved a step further, and saw the other side.

At the back of the head, another face was carved, staring out in the opposite direction. The long rippling hair was the same, merged with the hair of the first. But this face was startlingly different. There were the same clear-cut features, but now they were cold and stern; the mouth was a thin cruel line, and the eyes bored into Cally's with a dreadful chill menace that made her skin prickle with fear. Instinctively she moved aside, but the eyes seemed to follow, relentlessly holding her own.

Cally moved hastily backward to the mildness of the first stone face. But it no longer reassured her; she could not force out the image of the second, waiting on the other side. Then beyond the pillar, she caught sight of a figure standing some way off among the trees. It wore a blue cloak, with a hood pulled over the head: a bright shout of colour in the sombre wood. It stood very still, the dark opening of the hood turned towards Cally, as if it were watching her.

For a moment Cally felt cold with fright; she stood rigid, her fingernails digging into the palms of her hands. But the gentle stone face smiling at her from the pillar gave her confidence once more, and she took a deep breath.

'Hi!' she called, waving one arm at the cloaked figure. 'Hi!'

She moved forward, still waving – and suddenly the figure was no longer there.

Cally blinked. Her eyes had been fixed on the patch of blue, and she knew that it had not moved – and there was no cover among the small scrubby trees that could hide it. She paused, unhappy and irresolute, and glanced back at the pillar. Unexpectedly the fierce cold stare of the terrifying second face blazed full at her. Cally looked quickly away. Longing to run, she made herself walk deliberately away through the stunted pines, all the time feeling the stare of the cold stone eyes at her back, until the pillar was out of sight.

She was out in bright daylight now, under a sky filled with drifting clouds. Nearby, a great boulder twice her height rose from the scrubland. Feeling very small and alone, Cally sat down on the edge of the rock to rest. What would she do when night came if she were still wandering over this empty land? She felt in the pocket of her jeans, but produced nothing but a handkerchief, a stub of pencil and a broken comb. Shoving them despondently back again, she leant one hand on the rock – and jumped up at once as if she had been burned. Though this seemed a warm spring day, the surface of the giant boulder was cold as ice: terrifyingly cold, as if all the warmth of the air had been sucked out of it.

Staring at the rock, Cally backed slowly away from it, feeling once more a rising sense of unease, and the beginning of panic. As she watched, a ray of sunlight slanted briefly down from a break in the clouds. It rested on the boulder, brightening the smooth grey rock.

And there came suddenly a cracking, grinding sound, and a rumbling through the earth all around, and Cally saw the boulder move. She thought wildly of earthquakes, but the ground did not shake; instead the giant rock shifted and split and writhed apart, as if it were alive. Watching incredulously, she saw it take shape, two particular shapes, until suddenly there was no boulder at all but two huge figures, standing, turning to her.

For a moment she stood motionless, staring.

There were heads, limbs, bodies, but these were figures like nothing she could have imagined. They were neither human nor stone, but both together; they belonged to the earth and the empty land, and they were looking at her without eyes. Then they began to come towards her.

Cally ran. Choking with terror, she fled through the fern and brush, leaping over rocks, dodging trees; and all the time she heard a great slow tramping behind her, from the crashing stone feet of the two monstrous figures following. She dared not look over her shoulder. She ran and ran, gasping. whimpering and at last the brush thinned and she was running through long grass. and before her in a clearing stood a low stone house with smoke rising from its chimney. Through the terrible thudding behind her she heard again the strange rhythmic sound. more metallic now. that she had heard from far off. and near the house she saw a man swinging a long hammer up over his shoulder and down

For Cally he was the most welcome refuge she had ever seen. She raced towards him and he looked up. letting the hammer fall into a pile of rocks. He was tall and lean. wearing rough denim work-clothes: his face was deep-lined strong and almost ugly, with a shock of wiry black hair above. Skidding, she cannoned into his legs. Behind her. the great thudding steps slowed and came to a halt. The man caught her by the shoulders. Cally looked up at him in anguished appeal.

His face was expressionless. He set her upright and let her go. 'Why do you run?' he said. 'They will not hurt you.'

Cally's heart jumped; she felt cold. There was no refuge here. She had made a terrible mistake – but it was too late to draw back now.

The man looked out over her head. and raised his voice. 'Why do you bring this to me?'

Behind Cally. a huge rumbling voice spoke, deep, immensely strong. filling the air like the long growl of an avalanche.

'Did not mean to make afraid. Thought you might want.'

The man said irritably, 'For what?'

'For work. Did not mean. Girl – did not mean to make afraid.'

Cally stood trembling, her breath uneven. The man made a clicking sound with his tongue. impatient, and he took her again by the shoulders and spun her round. She flinched back against his knees. The two huge figures stood facing her. In the sunlight they were like rough misshapen sculp-

40

tures clumsily carved from great blocks of stone: arms without hands, legs without feet, heads without features. The slow rumbling voice came again from one of them.

'Did not mean . . .'

Even through her fear, Cally heard an incongruous note of appeal in the voice that for a wild moment reminded her of a small child apologizing. She swallowed.

'It's all right,' she said huskily. 'I'm . . . not afraid.'

'Hah!' said the man shortly, releasing her. 'Not afraid? You're shaking like an aspen. And were you running like the devil because you're not afraid?'

Cally said, 'It was – when they changed –'

'And if you don't understand, you fear.' He gave a brief snort of disgust, and turned to pick up his hammer. 'Just like Lugan's folk. Are you one of them?'

Cally said blankly, 'Who?'

'Where have you come from?'

'I – don't know. Another country.'

'Stonecutter,' said the deep creaking voice from the stone figure. 'We did wrong?'

'No, no,' said the black-haired man impatiently. 'She can work with Ryan. I dare say she needs a roof over her head.'

Cally thought of the dark wood, and the malevolent face on the pillar. In relief she smiled at him. 'Yes please.'

He looked at her coldly. 'Behind the house there is a door. Go through it, to the woman inside. Understand that here, life is work.'

Cally nodded, her smile fading.

'And understand one thing about the People, so that we'll have no more hysterics.' He pointed to the great stone creatures standing motionless before him. 'The sun wakes them. When the sun is gone, they . . . go to sleep. All of us here live by that rule, but for them it must be the touch of the sun that brings them back to life.'

41

Cally remembered the beam of sunlight on the grey rock. She said, 'The People?'

'It is what they call themselves.' The words were a dismissal; he turned away.

Cally glanced at the stone figures, but there was no way of telling if the blank faceless heads were looking back. She went to the house. Behind her, the thudding of the hammer began again – and with it a much more massive crashing, crunching sound, shaking the earth. Cally shivered, and did not turn to look.

The house was made of rough blocks of stone, set with small square windows deep in each wall, and roofed with blue slate. Cally found the heavy wooden door in the back wall, with a tall dark holly bush growing nearby. She knocked, timidly. Then she realized that the door was unlatched. Pushing, she found that it was in two halves; the top half swung open.

'No foot on the floor yet!' It was a quick, light voice, with a singing in its accent. Cally saw a broad, light-coloured floor, with heavy furniture all pushed into a cluster at one end of the room. By the fire in the big open hearth, a little woman with wispy grey hair caught up in a knot was kneeling with a bucket and a brush. She blinked up at Cally, in the sunlight from the doorway.

'Well, who is this now!' She stood up and padded across to the door; Cally saw that she had pieces of rag wrapped round each foot and tied at the ankles with string. The woman glanced down at them and laughed: an infectious, gurgling laugh, turning her small face into a maze of smiling wrinkled lines and rounding her cheeks like apples.

'It's the day for the floor, you see – no use washing it clean and then grubbying it up with your own feet, is there?'

'No.' Cally said, smiling. 'My mum walks about on dusters, when she's been polishing. That is – she used to.'

Her smile died suddenly, and she felt a choking in her throat.

The woman looked at her shrewdly, and reached out and gave her hand a quick light touch. But she asked no questions. 'Tired, you are,' she said. 'A cup of tea, and something to eat. But first I must finish my floor. What's your name?'

'Cally. He –' Cally gestured vaguely at the yard. 'He told me to come in here.'

'Oh yes,' the woman said comfortably. 'You would not be here if Stonecutter had not sent you in.'

'He said, she can work with Ryan.'

'That's me. And indeed you can.'

Cally said hesitantly, 'Mrs Ryan?'

'No, my dear, just Ryan. It is a shortening, of a name harder for the tongue.' She became brisk, looking round the room critically. 'Now let me see. I have the elder leaves, I need the dock. Do you know dock leaves?'

Cally was startled. 'Yes. The kind you rub on nettle stings?'

Ryan nodded approvingly. She reached to a shelf and took down a basket. 'Now do you go out there and bring me back four handfuls of good green dock. And – oh –' She reached again, and put a small dark pottery bowl in the basket. 'And a handful of sand.'

'Sand,' Cally said blankly.

'Easy to find. Where Stonecutter is, there's always sand.' She stood smiling at Cally like a small perky bird.

Baffled, Cally went back out into the sunshine with the basket. She turned away from the muffled thunder that was Stonecutter and the People at work, into a meadow beside the house. It stretched in a long lush sweep to the distant edge of the trees; as she wandered through the grass, she was puzzled, and did not know why. In a little while she realized: though trees and bushes and plants

43

grew luxuriantly everywhere around the house, nowhere could she see a single flower.

She found the broad dark-green leaves of dock easily in the long grass, growing in scattered clumps, and she filled the basket. Beyond the meadow, a huge stone wall twice her height stretched into the wood and out of sight; it seemed to have no purpose, enclosing nothing, marking no particular boundary. But it was newly-built, with trampled land and splintered young trees all around it. She imagined the clumsy crashing of the People, their handless arms raising great boulders into place, and shuddered. But she found sand for Ryan: silvery sand in little heaps all up and down the wall, from the crushing of the rock.

When she went back to the door of the house, fully open now, she paused at the step in surprise. All the grey-white floor was neatly patterned with criss-crossed strips of green; it was like a carpet. But it was not a carpet; she could see Ryan on her knees at the far corner of the room, making the last part of the pattern by rubbing a bunch of leaves hard against the floor so that they left a green stain.

Ryan looked up. 'Good! Just in time! There's the elder done – now the dock, to finish it.' And Cally saw that round the edge of the floor she had left a blank space about a foot wide.

She said, 'It's pretty.'

'And useful,' Ryan said a trifle grimly, but she did not explain what she meant. 'Now do you come in with that sand, and sprinkle it all evenly across here.' She pointed to the broad hearthstone in front of the fire, which she had scrubbed clean of ash and soot.

Cally came in, stepping carefully between the green patterning. Obediently she sprinkled the hearthstone, then sat watching, still and silent, as Ryan finished rubbing her pattern with the dock leaves round the edge of the floor. The old woman heaved herself to her feet. She looked tired, her face more lined.

'Now the last thing.'

Crossing to the hearth, she took from the mantel a slab of blue stone the size of her fist; kneeled again and began rubbing it on the sanded surface, slowly, deliberately. She drew lines of crosses, crossed each with another cross, then swept the sand away with a brush so that the pattern stood out clear and blue on the hearth.

'There,' she said, sitting back on her heels. 'Safe for a month, now. No need to keep from walking on it, child – it will stay and stay.'

'Safe?' Cally said.

'Protected,' Ryan said, biting off the word like a piece of thread; her small lined face was suddenly secret, enclosed. She had Cally help her pull back the heavy wooden chairs and table piled against the wall; then she poured two mugs of steaming fragrant tea from a big brown teapot. She gave Cally one, with a plateful of small flat cakes speckled with currants.

Sitting down, she said abruptly, 'Where are you going?'

Cally said, 'I don't know.' She hesitated. 'If I were in my own world, I'd be going to a place by the sea where my parents are. Only – I don't think they'd be there any more.' She looked down at her cup, unseeing.

'The sea links all worlds,' Ryan said gently. 'But Stonecutter would set you to work?'

For a moment Cally was silent, lost; then she looked up. 'I'm sorry. Yes, that's what he said.' She sipped her tea. 'This smells so good. Like raspberries.'

'Raspberry and camomile,' Ryan said absently. She was looking at Cally, but her creased-about eyes were blank, as if she saw only her own mind. 'You must not stay long,' she said, 'or he will never let you go He will keep you for her.'

45

The tea and cakes were making Cally feel herself again She said, puzzled, 'Her?'

'She who brought you here. She whose land this is.' Ryan pointed at Cally's mug. 'Take your cup to the door, child, and do what I shall tell you. I will give you more tea in a moment. Now.'

There was a sudden urgency in the word. Cally got up, wondering and crossed to the open door.

'Swirl the cup twice, and throw out the tea on to the ground. Then bring the cup back to me.'

Dutifully Cally tossed the golden liquid out of the mug; it glittered for a moment in the sunshine as it fell. But in the same moment she paused, arrested, staring out across the clearing to the edge of the straggling trees. There was a patch of bright blue against the green, unmistakable: the blue of the hooded figure she had seen in the wood.

She blinked – and nothing was there.

Ryan said, 'What's the matter?'

'Nothing.' Cally brought her the mug, patterned inside now with the broad wet leaves left by the tea. Ryan set it on her dark woollen skirt and peered inside, turning it slowly in both hands.

'Yes. Two gone, and a travelling . . . And another traveller, to go by your side. A tower by the lake, a tower full of dreams and danger. And the sea, yes, and – now what is that –?'

She broke off, and looked up at Cally with a curious new expression on her small seamed face: a mixture of pleasure and surprise and a kind of wariness. She said, 'Show me your hands.'

Cally hesitated, then reluctantly held out her hands, palm upward. 'They're . . . not very pretty,' she said.

Ryan gazed at the thickened, horny skin on each palm, tracing it gently with a forefinger. 'Yes,' she said softly, but

46

it was not an answer. 'Well, well . . . yes . .' Her bright eyes flickered up to Cally's 'Did your mother sing?'

'Yes,' said Cally in astonishment. 'How did you know? She used to sing to me when –' She stopped, suddenly remembering the voice that had been like her mother's and yet not like.

And all at once, in the same moment, the air was full of singing; it was back again. the high sweet wordless music that had driven her from that world into this. But it was gentle now, as it had been at the first; soft, beckoning. And it was not in the room or in the house. but outside, in the sunshine and the trees.

Cally turned instinctively to look out – and found herself face to face with a hooded figure in a blue robe, framed against the sky in the doorway, looking in.

Chapter VI

Cally gasped, and jumped backwards away from the door. Beside her Ryan was standing stiff and tense, all the smiling lines of her face drawn straight. She was gazing at the figure in hostile challenge.

'You may not come in,' she said.

The blue-robed figure raised one hand, and the music that filled the air died away. Then the hand went to the deep folds of the hood and pulled it down, and Cally saw that it was a woman who stood there. Against the bright sky her face was lost in shadow, but the sun blazed in her hair as if it were spun glass.

'Oho,' she said softly, looking down at the green-patterned floor. 'Rhiannon, daughter of the Roane, you are not welcoming.'

Ryan said, unmoving, 'Nor shall I ever be.'

'Not even for the sake of our Cally here?' The woman purposely moved so that the sunlight fell on her, and Cally caught her breath. It was the lined pale face, blue-eyed, old yet ageless, of the woman who had come to take her father away.

Ryan said in warning, 'It is the Lady Taranis. Do not listen to her.'

'But I know her,' Cally said. 'She took my father away to a hospital, by the sea. And my mother, to be with him.' She came forward eagerly. 'Have you seen her? Is she all right?'

'Everything is all right,' Taranis said, but she was looking past Cally, at Ryan, and there was a coldness in her blue eyes. She said sharply, 'Do not hinder me. You have not the power.'

'I have the power,' Ryan said. 'This is my house.'

'But you are in my country – which none can leave without my willing it. As you know, Rhiannon.' She smiled, and there was a hint of malice in the smile that made Cally uneasy. But then the blue eyes were on hers again, shining with warmth. 'Come with me, Cally. I will take you to the sea, to your mother and your father, and you will be safe again. All together.'

Cally felt Ryan take her hand; small strong fingers, holding fast. 'She will go,' Ryan said. 'But in her own time, and her own way.'

Cally could feel the force of Taranis' nature reaching out for her like a wave. 'Come,' said the soft coaxing voice. 'Cally, come with me.'

'Do not move,' Ryan said in her ear. 'But hold out your hand to her, and ask her to take it.'

'Come,' said the Lady Taranis.

Cally reached out her hand. She said nervously, 'Here.'

Ryan said again at her ear, the lilt of her accent very strong now, 'The patterning that I was telling you, the greening of the floor, it is a protection against all harm. None who would work harm may cross it. So now you may see.'

Taranis smiled at Cally. 'First you must come out.'

Cally said nothing, but stood motionless with her hand outstretched, and Taranis' pale beautiful face grew angry. For an instant she made as if to move forward, but it was as if she were on the other side of a glass wall, invisibly held back. Glaring at Ryan, she flung round towards the yard, her blue cloak swirling, and she called in a high clear voice, 'Stonecutter!'

He came with a great rumbling and shaking of the earth, the huge faceless forms of the People around him.

'What have you been doing?' she said.

He looked at her without emotion. 'Building walls.'

'Build one round this house!' said Taranis fiercely. 'Keep your Rhiannon inside it for ever!'

'I mean to,' Stonecutter said.

Ryan's fingers tightened on Cally's hand. From the figures outside there rose a long deep murmur like the sound of a gigantic swarm of bees, and Cally realized with a chill that there must be far more of them out there now than before

'As for the girl,' Taranis said, 'I shall come back for her.'

There was a flicker like the shadow of a bird crossing the sun, and a quiver of high singing voices too brief to catch, and in the next moment she was no longer there.

Ryan's fingers relaxed. Stonecutter came in through the doorway 'Is supper ready?' he said, as if nothing had happened

'It will be when you are washed. Come, Cally.' The old woman turned, with a quick swish of her long dark skirt like a girl moving, and Stonecutter went outside again; Cally heard from the side wall of the house the creaking metallic sound of a pump, and water splashing. Ryan was stirring a pot on the stove; she gestured for Cally to fetch plates from a shelf.

Cally said urgently, 'But my mother and father – where are they? What will she do?'

'Nothing. They are safe from her now Be patient for a little child – we cannot talk yet.'

In silence, they ate a stew of meat and unfamiliar vegetables with some strange sweet-tasting greens which Cally to her surprise, wolfed down as eagerly as the meat. 'This is good!' she said.

Ryan smiled at her.

'You baked no bread today,' Stonecutter said, chewing; his lean face was dour and preoccupied. He offered no thanks ever, nor gave Ryan any word of praise; watching him, Cally wondered if he had ever smiled.

'It was the day for the floor,' Ryan said.

'You are a fool to make your patterning. It does no good – the power of the land is all hers. Why make her angry?'

Ryan said quietly, 'I will not be her creature. Or yours.'

'Nor will you leave,' he said. 'The wall is already there – the People have seen to that.'

Cally turned in her chair to look out at the yard. All round the house, out at the edge of the trees, the massive stone figures had been standing in a silent ominous line. Now the sun was going down, and the shadow of the trees had overtaken them – and where they had stood, there was now a long unbroken barrier of rock.

Ryan said, 'It is not your walls that keep me here.'

Stonecutter shrugged. 'The door has always been open, if you had cared to . . . leave things behind. Perhaps the wall is for the girl.'

Cally stood up suddenly. 'Please let me go,' she said.

He looked at her with dismissive surprise, as if the chair had spoken. 'I offered shelter, and you took it. And the Lady Taranis chooses to have you stay. It is almost sundown – go to bed.'

Cally opened her mouth to argue, but Ryan took her hand firmly again and led her to a mattress close to her own bed in the back room of the house. 'I will wake you ' she said in a whisper.

But Cally woke of her own accord, in the darkness, to the sound of Ryan's soft breathing and the glimmer of moonlight on the wall. She had been dreaming, she knew, but in the moment that she woke the dream flickered away and would not come back; she knew only that it had woken her, like a calling.

She lay there miserable and lost, clutching the blankets

round her. Everything that had been firm and certain in her life seemed to have melted away like spring snow: her home, her parents, even the awareness of herself, like a reflection in a mirror, that she had always had inside. She thought; *I don't know who I am, I don't know what to do* – and there was an ache in her throat, and she wept silently into the rough linen pillow.

But something in her mind said obstinately: *You are Cally. You can do anything you want to do.* Gradually the tears stopped, and she found herself thinking of the coldness of the Stonecutter and the warmth of Ryan, and of Ryan's admonition: *you must not stay long.* And with a chill of fright and excitement she knew that she must go, now; leave this house which threatened to hold her forever, and go out into the enchanted country through which she did not know her way.

Quietly she slipped out of bed, took off the soft voluminous nightgown Ryan had given her, and put on her clothes and shoes. Then she tiptoed out into the front room, where moonlight shafted brightly in through the window, turning the floor to white patterned with black – and she stopped stock-still. On a mattress near the hearth, Stonecutter lay sleeping, wrapped in blankets; she could see the shape of his head, and the angle of his knees. Very slowly, inch by inch, she edged sideways so that she could pass around his feet. But the space was narrow between mattress and wall, and she was no more than halfway when she overbalanced. As she toppled, her foot came forward and struck Stonecutter's legs, and she cried out in terror – not for fear of having woken him, but for a greater fear. The body that she had kicked was not human; it was hard as stone.

Ryan's voice said compassionately behind her. 'Yes. I would have spared you that. He does not need the warmth of the sunshine to waken him, like the People, but from sundown to sunup he is stone, as they are.'

Cally shrank back from the still figure, terrified that she might glimpse what lay under the blankets. Ryan put an arm round her; she was dressed in a full, warm nightgown like the one she had lent Cally, and her grey hair was long and loose over her shoulders. Looking at her face in the moonlight, Cally realized that she was not a very old woman at all, and that the network of lines had been put there by care, not by age.

She said, 'Why?'

'The Lady Taranis is a jealous mistress,' Ryan said wearily. 'Once a long time ago he fell in love, and she was angry, and made sure that he would never sleep with his lover. And to take care of the days, she touched his heart with stone as well.'

She looked down sadly at Stonecutter.

Cally said, 'Why do you stay?'

The sadness went out of Ryan's face, and left it empty. She said, 'I came here because he had something of mine without which I can never be free. And he has it shut under stone as cold as his heart, and I cannot leave without it.' She smiled ruefully at Cally, and gave her shoulder a squeeze as she released her. 'But I am used to waiting. You are not – you are young. Were you running away?'

Cally nodded.

'Not yet,' Ryan said. 'Not while the moon is up. The moonlight belongs to Taranis – you must never forget that. While it shines, unless you are under a roof, she can turn your will to do anything she wants you to do. But in the sunlight, even in this her land, you will always have a choice.'

Holding up her skirt to step lightly over the still figure on the floor, she crossed to the door, unbolted its top half and swung it open. 'Half a moon,' she said, looking out. 'And an hour more to its setting. Then it will be half-light, owl-light, the light between the dawn and the rising of the sun, and

53

then you may go – when the night no longer obeys Taranis. and the day has not yet woken the People. I will dress and wait with you, and we will make ourselves some raspberry tea.'

Cally followed her to the door. 'I wish you'd come with me.'

'I would if I could,' Ryan said. She stood looking out at the shadowed grey-white moonlit world, and she put up her hands to hold each side of the door-frame, so that with her arms wide it was as if she were speaking to it all. She said softly, 'There are no birds here, as there are no animals in the wood, because the coldness of Stonecutter keeps them away. But there are birds in the sky and the trees and the grass, beyond the building of Stonecutter's walls. They are the birds of Rhiannon, and they will go with you, and comfort you, and help you to the sea.'

Standing there unmoving, she turned her young-old face and smiled, with the same gaiety suddenly that Cally had seen when she first came to the house. 'Remember, child. This is all I have to give you, to help you on your way. If you are in great trouble ever, or in danger, or in emptiness of spirit, call on the birds of Rhiannon of the Roane.'

Cally said in a whisper, 'Rhiannon of the Roane. Ryan.'

Ryan said, 'And when you reach the sea, go to the rocks, and give a message to the one who will be waiting. Say: do not despair. She will come.'

'Who will be waiting?' Cally said.

'You will know, because he will know you. By your hands.' Ryan stepped back from the door-frame and held out her hands, palms upward. And on each palm Cally saw the same strange horny growth of skin that was on her mother's hands, and on her own.

When the moon was gone, and the sky grey with the beginnings of dawn, Ryan made Cally put on a warm woven jacket, and carry a bag of tough burlap on her shoulder. 'A change of clothes,' she said. 'And some food.' She opened the door. The air was cold.

'Over the wall,' Ryan said. 'It will not hinder you, if you touch without fear. They will be no more than rocks, until the sun comes up. Then you must go straight, as straight as you can – follow the morning star. And you will come to a stream. Follow the water always, and it will take you in the end to the sea.'

She put an arm round Cally's shoulders. Cally gave her a quick hug, and set off across the yard without looking back. She knew that if she turned, she might not have the courage to go at all.

Before her the stone wall loomed, dark and ominous in the colourless early-morning world. It was twice her height Cally hesitated, hearing again in her mind the great crack·ing, grinding sound of the huge boulder coming alive, becoming the People. Suppose Taranis had bewitched them so that they would not need the sun; suppose they might come alive at her touch . . .?

Clutching the pack Ryan had given her, she made herself march up to the wall and touch it. The rock was ice-cold, as the boulder had been the day before; but it was only rock. Nothing moved; no sound came. And now that she was close, she saw that the barrier was not smooth and vertical like a real wall, but mounded, uneven – so uneven that she scrambled over it with no need even to look for footholds.

Then she was down in the grass on the other side. Low in the grey sky ahead of her, above a straggling line of trees, a single star shone white and steady. Cally set off towards it. Soon she was among the trees, and when she looked back, she could no longer see the wall.

She walked for a long time through the grass and scrub and the small trees. Behind her the sun came up, and suddenly there was colour all around: the grey sky became

55

blue, the leaves were green. The star had disappeared, but for direction now she tried always to keep the sun at her back.

Sometimes she crossed sweeping areas of bracken, the tough green fronds as high as her waist, so that she was wading through a rustling green sea. In the beginning, she often came upon Stonecutter's fallen, forgotten walls, winding apparently aimlessly through bracken and grass, sometimes with trees growing through them. But after a while she found no more.

Once, she saw a little way off a tall grey pillar like the one she had seen before, and she thought she saw the shaping of the two faces carved at its peak. But she looked away at once, and took care to walk wide of it. She knew very well, now, whose two faces the statues wore.

Gradually the trees began to change; more and more often Cally saw the dancing leaves and the smooth grey trunks of beech, with dark mounds of rhododendrons growing between. In the soft green light she felt easier, without the tense awareness of danger that had been tight around her like a rope. Nearby, a startled squirrel ran up a tree and perched on a branch, scolding her, and she realized that the air around her was no longer silent, but full of the murmur of birds.

The wood was cool, and she found it hard to make sure that the sun, climbing higher beyond the leaves, was at her back. But soon, close by, she heard a new sound: the gentle rhythmic rippling of a stream. In her mind she heard Ryan's voice: *Follow the water, and it will take you in the end to the sea.*

It was a pretty stream, running unhurried through the wood, with moss pillowed on its banks, and a fringe of broad sedge grasses and strands of watercress. Cally followed it for a long time, winding through the trees. Small birds fluttered and chirped in the branches over her head, but she could never catch a clear sight of them. Then the water seemed to quicken, and the stream ran straight. Bright sky gleamed through the trees ahead, and almost before Cally realized it, she was out in the sunshine, standing on a high bank overlooking a lake.

The dark water stretched before her still as glass, a broad expanse broken only by the overlapping V-shaped wakes of two ducks swimming slowly into the distance. Far out, she could see the opposite bank, fringed with trees – and closer, in the middle of the lake, the wooded green mound of an island, with a rocky cliff from which a tall stone tower rose.

Cally stared at the tower. It was like a piece of a medieval castle: square, crenellated, with deep slit windows just visible in the walls. Its grey surface shone in the sunlight; suddenly she wanted very much to be inside it, to look out over the water and the trees from those high battlements. But there was no way to the island from the bank where she stood.

Then the still surface of the lake was broken again. Gliding out from behind the island came a small dinghy, with a boy standing in its stern working a single oar to and fro. The water rippled out behind the boat in a long V, like the wake of the ducks, with a line of wavelets in the centre from the sculling oar. She saw the boy pause as if in surprise, looking up at the tower.

Without stopping to think, Cally put two fingers in her mouth and blew a piercing whistle; her father had shown her how, years before, before he became ill and forgot his habit of teaching her – on principle - tricks generally thought unsuitable for girls. For a moment she found herself remembering the way he had made her learn to throw a knife, and to cast with a fly-rod: much more fun than her mother's gentle instruction in how to sew and knit and cook.

The boy's head jerked round. Cally whistled again, and waved. The boat changed direction, and began moving towards her over the still dark water of the lake.

Chapter VII

Sculling to the shore, Westerly realized with astonishment and some confusion that the figure scrambling down the bank towards him was a girl. He sighed. Nothing in this country could be relied upon to be what it seemed.

Overhead in the blue sky, a small hawk hovering over the island dropped suddenly in a long vertical dive, and disappeared into the trees behind the tower.

Westerly let the bow of the boat crunch against the shore. 'Need a lift?' he said.

She looked all right, at any rate: straight brown hair. clear. dark-lashed grey eyes under a high forehead, a delicate mouth but a chin that looked as if it knew how to be obstinate.

Cally in her turn saw a brown-skinned boy about her own age and height, with dark hair and eyes, grinning at her amiably. There was a long rip in the sleeve of his rather dirty white shirt. She grasped the bow of the boat.

'Are you going to that tower?' she said.

'I was thinking about it. Hop in. No charge for residents.'

She clambered in. 'I'm not a resident. I never saw it till a minute ago.'

'Join the club. Neither did I. You'll have to come further up this way, or I can't get the bow off.'

Cally wobbled back towards him. The boat swayed.

'Careful,' he said.

'Sorry.'

'Can you swim?'

'No,' Cally said sorrowfully.

'In that case, be *very* careful.'

She sat obediently still on a thwart, balancing herself. 'I'm Cally.'

'Westerly.' He pushed the boat out with the oar.

'What a funny name,' Cally said.

He looked at her sideways, raising one eyebrow.

Cally said in confusion, 'Well, yes. But it used to be worse They christened me Calliope.'

Westerly said, sculling back across the lake, 'There was a boy in my class called Angel.'

'What did you call him?'

'All kinds of things. Here, sit in the stern – this isn't working. I'd better row.'

As he set both oars in the rowlocks Cally said abruptly. 'You don't belong here either, do you?'

'No,' Westerly said. He thought of adding more, but could think of nothing simple. He started to row. 'Tell me if I'm headed wrong.'

'Pull on your right a bit. Where are you going?'

'Didn't you say to the tower?'

'Yes. No – I mean, are you on your way somewhere?'

Westerly hesitated; then decided there could be no guile in a girl who could whistle like a boy. 'Seaward,' he said.

'What?'

'To the sea.'

Cally looked up at him sharply. 'So am I.'

'Then why are we going to this tower?'

'You're nearly there. Pull left. Now both. I don't know. I think I'm supposed to. Something somebody said –' She thought: *I can't tell him Ryan saw it in the tea-leaves.* 'Stop. Here's the shore.'

Westerly turned, and they were both silent as they looked up at the tower. On its rocky base it reared up over them into the blue sky, vast, mysterious; they could see the outlines of the huge stone blocks from which it was made. Nothing stirred anywhere.

Westerly shouted suddenly, 'Hey! Anybody home?'

His voice echoed back at them across the lake. *'Home . . . home . . . home . . .'* No sound came from the tower.

'Let's have one of those oars,' Cally said. She poked it over the stern and pushed, and the dinghy nosed up on a small sandy beach. They climbed out and pulled it clear of the water.

The sand of the beach was grey, filled with small white flakes that glittered in the sun. Broken branches and twigs littered the waterline. Westerly pulled his pack out of the boat and swung it up on his back; he looked at Cally striding long-legged up the beach with her own, and wondered what drew her to the tower. The urge to explore was strong in him too, but he felt a wariness beneath it, a sense that something perilous waited here.

Cally called over her shoulder, 'There are steps!'

He caught up with her. The grey rock was like a cliff before them, but carved diagonally into it was a huge stairway, winding upwards, each step higher than his knee.

He reached one leg up to the first step. 'Look at the size of them! Must have been made for a giant.'

Cally looked at him quickly, and he laughed. 'Jack and the Beanstalk? Not really. Come on.'

They heaved themselves up the stairs, scuffling through dirt and sand and dead leaves. As the stairway curved, biting into the rock, its sides cut them off; they could see nothing but the rocky walls, the rising steps and a strip of sky overhead. Silence enclosed them.

Cally said, climbing, 'That crack about Jack and the Beanstalk . . . There *are* weird things in this place. Including giants – sort of.'

'I know there are,' Westerly said. He reached for the next step. 'I just wasn't sure you did. No more cracks, okay?'

'Okay,' Cally said.

Then they were out in the air again, breathless, the wind

loud in their ears; they were at the top of the steps, standing on a rough rocky platform, and before them was a massive stone door. It was set close against the granite blocks of the tower wall: a blue-grey slab of slate, straight-edged, smooth as paper.

Westerly considered it. 'No handle, no door-knocker. No way in. Just a big chunk of slate saying Go Away.'

Cally stared at the door, disappointed. 'Maybe I was wrong about the tower. Maybe we aren't supposed to go inside.'

In the same moment there was a deep rumbling, grating sound, and the tall slate door began to move sideways. They could feel it grinding against the rock beneath their feet. Caught in amazement they stood watching, until it stopped, leaving a gaping doorway with only darkness visible inside.

Nervously Cally took hold of Westerly's sleeve; but it was she who stepped forward. He said swiftly, 'No!'

'Why not?' She was at the edge of the doorway, peering in; then she let go of his sleeve and said gaily, 'Oh *look* –' and she was inside. At once the grinding rumble of rock began again, and the door started to slide back.

Westerly said in horror, 'Cally!' For a paralysed instant he paused, staring at the moving door; then he dived after her and slipped inside. With an echoing crash the door shut behind them.

'Where are you?'

Then he saw that the tower was not dark. They stood in a square, high-ceilinged room walled with the same rough granite blocks, and in the middle of the room hung a strange white sphere, glowing with cold light. It hovered, shifting gently, like a great white ball held up by an invisible stream of air. But it was not hanging, and it was not held up. It was simply there.

Westerly gazed at it, fascinated; then moved slowly forward.

'Don't touch it!' It was Cally's turn to hold back. But

before he was close, the ball seemed silently to explode, and the curious white light was all around them in the room like mist. They heard a new rumbling of stone, and before them on the far wall two tall stone slabs slid sideways, revealing two staircases. One led upward, the other down.

The slabs quivered and were still, and the room was silent again. The white mist all round them hovered about the gap in the wall, lapping at its edges.

Westerly peered into the blackness beyond. 'Well, do we go up, or down?'

'Up sounds better.' Cally peered past him at the ascending stone steps; they disappeared round a bend. 'Only – it's so dark.'

But as they stepped through the opening on to the stairs, the white mist poured after them, following, transforming the slanting stairway into a tunnel of white light. The stairs rose steeply; then suddenly the inner wall ended and they were in an open space like a kind of landing. The mist-light flowed out around them, and at either end of the landing wall they saw a heavy wooden door.

Westerly groaned. 'Always doors. It's like one of those puzzles – a box in a box in a box.'

He looked for a handle on the nearest door, but again there was nothing; no sign anywhere of handle or keyhole or latch. Leaning his shoulder against it, he pushed hard, but the door did not budge. Baffled, he ran his fingers over the heavy time-rutted wood.

'It's ancient – look at those cracks. And cobwebs on the hinges ... nobody's been through here for years and years.'

Cally was silent. He glanced at her; she was staring upward, her face tight and pale. She said huskily, 'Look at that!'

Above the door, carved into the stone wall, dusty and worn with age, he saw the word: CALLIOPE.

Cally said, in the same strange husky voice, 'I think I know how to get in.'

She held up both hands and put her palms against the surface of the wood, and instantly at her touch the heavy door swung quietly open.

The room was full of sunlight, pouring in through broad windows. One window was open, and white curtains shifted gently in the breeze. On three sides, smooth plastered walls were painted from floor to ceiling with a single unbroken picture: green water, white waves, a golden shore and a blue sky.

The fourth wall, in which the door was set, was full of books: the shelves too ran from floor to ceiling, and a neat white ladder was set beside them to put the highest books within reach. The floor was carpeted in soft gold wool, and beside the open window was a bed covered with a quilt patterned in bright flowers. A white chair stood at a desk made of light bleached wood, and in the mirror of a small dressing-table Westerly could see the reflection of the blue sky. He was not sure whether it was the sky outside the tower, or the sky painted on the walls.

He looked again at Cally's tense face. 'Are you all right?'

Cally stood in the middle of the room. She said shakily 'When I was little, I always wanted my bedroom walls to be white, so that I could paint a mural all over them. A picture of the sea and the sky, with a sandy beach. I've never seen the sea – only pictures ... And I wanted a wall full of shelves for all my books, and a desk like that one, and a mirror like –' She swallowed. 'Is the frame of that mirror carved?'

Westerly crossed to look. 'Yes,' he said, wondering. Carved all round the edge, with little fishes, and flowers and leaves.'

Cally nodded. 'And over here there's a closet, with a door

63

you can't see. With the slow, abstracted certainty of a sleepwalker she moved to the painted wall beside the bed. reached to a white curling wave and pulled at a ring her fingers found there, and a section of the mural swung out as a door. Inside, Westerly saw a closet filled with bright dresses hanging in a row, and shelves of neatly folded blouses and scarves, with a rack of shoes underneath.

Cally reached up for a dress on a hanger. 'There's the prettiest, the blue silk one, with the ribbon belt.' She looked at it for a moment. expressionless, then put it back.

Westerly said, 'Is it a copy of your room at home?'

Cally stared at him. 'Of course not. I've never seen anything like it. It's the room I dreamed about having. And everything in it. All the things I hoped I might have one day ... some day ... There's my own bathroom too. behind another secret door in that wall.' She pointed, but did not move.

Westerly looked at her for a long moment. Then he went out of the room, back to the landing. The white light-mist had retreated down the stairs, as if driven back by the sunlight; it lay in a pool, five or six steps down.

With Cally slowly following, Westerly crossed to the second of the two tall wooden doors. He looked up, and saw written over the lintel in the same worn, carved letters: WESTERLY. Glancing at Cally, he set his palms against the surface of the door and pushed.

The door did not open.

Cally said hesitantly, 'That worked for me – but I think maybe you have to do something that's specially yours.'

'Hum,' Westerly said. He thought for a moment. Then he swung down the pack from his back, and took out a long knife. Cally recoiled a little as he pulled it from its sheath. As she watched, Westerly flicked the knife sharply forward so that the blade hung quivering in the age-worn wood of the door. and he said. low and fast. some words that she did not hear.

The door swung open and Westerly stepped through it - and disappeared.

Chapter VIII

Cally stood staring at the open door. She could see nothing beyond it but a grey haze. There was no sign of a room; no outline of walls or ceiling or floor. *No floor . . .*

Anxiously she lunged forward, reaching for the door-jamb, with a sudden terrible image of Westerly stepping into space, falling the height of the tower to stone beneath. But a barrier met her, throwing her backward. It was as if she had come up against a glass wall; yet she had touched nothing solid, there was nothing there. Again she tried to move to the doorway, and again she was held back, power-less. She remembered how the Lady had been held, trying in vain to break through the force that kept her from Ryan's protected house, and she thought miserably: *but I don't mean any harm . . .*

There was no sound in the tower; the silence pressed in on Cally as if it had weight. Fear came trickling cold into her mind; she thought of the immense slate door below, shutting out the world, and of the dark stair they had not taken, winding down into unknown depths. Would she dare go down there alone?

She called out desperately to the open door and the grey space, 'Oh Westerly, come back!' There was only the silence swallowing her voice, and the light slanting out from the door of the room at the other end of the landing: the room with her name written over its door.

All at once that room seemed a refuge, beckoning her with its familiar dream-images. Cally turned and made her way slowly back to the other door, hearing her steps echo

round the rough stone walls. She came into the glow of the
sunlight beaming out from the room, and just as she was
about to go in, she heard Westerly's voice behind her.

'Cally? You all right?'

She spun round, relief and fury tumbling over one another
in her mind. 'Where were you?'

Westerly came towards her, his pack slung over one
shoulder. His dark hair was falling over his forehead; his
brown face was unsmiling, preoccupied, as if part of him
were a long way away. He said again, 'You all right?'

'I'm fine.'

'How long was I gone?'

'Just a few minutes, I suppose. It seemed like a month.
What happened?'

Westerly pushed his hair out of his eyes, and the look of
preoccupation left his face as if he had pushed that away
too. He said suddenly, irrelevantly, 'I'm *hungry*.'

Cally remembered the bag Ryan had given her. 'I've got
some food.'

Westerly followed her into the sunlit room and stood in
the middle of the floor, looking round at the sea-painted
walls. He said slowly, as if he were feeling for words, 'These
rooms are dreams, I think. This one – you said it was everything you'd always wanted.'

Cally had found two thick sandwiches of meat and bread
at the top of the pack; she held one out to him. 'Yes. And
nobody had ever known those things but me.'

Westerly sat down beside her on the broad window-seat
and bit into his sandwich. 'But where you came from, you
did have a room of your own?'

Cally nodded, her mouth full.

'I didn't,' Westerly said. He looked at the wall again. 'My
mother and I lived in two rooms, in a house with five other
families. One room was for cooking and living, the other
was for sleeping – we had a curtain down the middle of it, to

67

separate the beds and make believe each of them was alone. But they weren't – no one was ever alone. Only in summer, outdoors, when we went out of the city to the river, and I could fish or just roam about.'

He took another huge bite and sat chewing reflectively. Cally watched him, curious. There was something in his face that made it unlike any she had ever seen: the high cheekbones clear under the tanned skin, perhaps, or the jet-black pupils of the eyes.

Westerly said, 'I wanted that more than anything – to be alone sometimes. Private – in a place where nobody else in the world could come.' He glanced at Cally with a quick apologetic grin. 'And I went through that door into my dream, and that was what I found.'

'Were you *in* that room?'

'Of course. It was wonderful. But most of all I was .. separate.'

'You sure were,' Cally said ruefully. She looked at her sandwich, then let her hand drop in her lap. 'Westerly – where *are* we?'

He chewed. 'Don't know about you, but I'm travelling.'

Cally stared at him. 'How can you just say that? It's a different world we're in, it's . . . it doesn't make any sense. I mean one moment I was in –'

'Stop!' Westerly said.

Cally blinked at him, startled.

'I don't want to know where you come from,' he said. The black eyes were distanced, wary. 'And where I come from . . . doesn't matter. Let's just leave that out of it.'

'I wasn't bringing it in,' Cally said frostily.

'Don't be upset,' he said. 'I have to be careful, that's all. There's someone – something – following me. And everything here is so . . . there are some things you mustn't even *say*. Until you know what the place is – and I don't know any more than you do.' He looked at her wide eyes, and felt repentant. 'Tell me how you got here.'

'I came through a mirror,' Cally said.

There was a pause.

Westerly said, 'Why?'

'It's crazy!' Cally said desperately. 'People can't walk through mirrors.'

'Of course they can't,' he said. 'But why did you?'

'I was . . . I was trying to get away.' She pulled herself very upright and sat still, remembering. 'My father was dying. He had a muscle disease they can't cure, he'd been ill for months. He went away to a special hospital, by the sea somewhere, and my mother sort of . . . faded, and she went after him. I think she was ill too but wouldn't tell me. They never liked talking about bad things. Now I think maybe they're both dead.'

She was silent for a moment. Westerly said quietly, 'I'm sorry.'

'I was on my own in the house,' Cally said, 'and I heard this . . . music. Like Ma singing. Only it wasn't her.' She paused again, and Westerly saw her hands clench in her lap. 'I'm sure it wasn't her. It was awful, I was terrified. And I was standing near her mirror and I reached my hands out to it, and it – let me through. And I was here. In a wood.'

She stopped, and sat silent again. Then she said, 'I'm going to the sea, to find them. If they're alive. I know that's where they must be, different world or not.'

Westerly pulled a flask of water out of his pack, and gave it to her. 'I don't remember my father,' he said. 'Maybe he's alive, somewhere. My mother said they kept him on an island. They took him away when I was a baby.'

Cally stared. 'They?'

'The army,' Westerly said. 'They run things, where I come from. My mother got away, with me. The city's like an ant hill, you can just live like ants and not be noticed. She

69

always said they'd catch up with us one day though – and they did. It took them sixteen years. They wanted me, my mother said.'

'Why would they want you?' Cally said.

Westerly looked at her gravely. 'Thanks a lot,' he said.

Cally flushed. 'I'm sorry, I didn't mean –'

He was grinning. 'Why would the army want an ant? I don't know. Maybe they thought I'd go into politics, like my father.' The grin faded, as though it had never been really there. and Cally saw lines round his eyes and mouth that did not belong on the face of a boy. 'So they came after me.' he said. 'But it was her they killed.'

The room was very quiet.

'There were three black cars out in the street one day.' Westerly said. 'And a hammering at the door. My mother made me push a table against the door, and when I turned round again she'd pulled down an old rug that had always hung on the wall, and there was another little door behind it that I'd never seen before. She said, "Don't ask questions, do what I tell you. You must close your eyes and open that door, go through it, count to three and open your eyes. Then pick up what you will find waiting, and wherever you may find yourself, however strange or terrible things may seem, go on, as far and as fast as you can. Travelling. Seaward, to your father."

'I couldn't understand what it was all about. I said, "I'm not going anywhere without you." She wasn't listening, she said, "Tell no one where you come from, and trust only three –"' He broke off; his face was closed, inturned. He took the flask from Cally and began turning it in his hands.

'They were still hammering at the door.' he said, 'and they yelled that they'd shoot if we didn't open up. I was scared. I grabbed at her to pull her out of the way. But I was too late. They fired a burst through the door and it hit her full on. Slantwise across her chest. Knocked her back against

70

the wall. She was dead before she knew anything. I've seen people dead before, but – but it was *her* –'

Cally stared at him in horrified silence. He was looking straight ahead at the wall. She reached out a hand to him and then let it drop again; the inadequacy seemed too great.

Westerly's voice was calm, empty. 'I think I screamed, he said. 'I went out of my head for a minute. I wanted to kill them, I picked up a chair because it was the only thing I could see, and then I remembered my knife, and I pulled that out. They had something heavy now, they were hitting the lock where they'd shot at it. I looked at my mother lying there with her eyes open and blood all over her, and although she was dead I swear I heard her voice from somewhere, very loud, very strong, filling the room, filling my whole head. *Do what I tell you . . . however strange or terrible things may seem, do what I tell you . . .* So I did. I put down the chair and I closed my eyes and went through the little door in the wall. I could hear the crashing as they broke the other door in. I closed my door and counted three, and there was no sound at all from the other side then, just birds singing, and a wind blowing. And when I opened my eyes I was standing somewhere I'd never seen, high up on open moorland with a track leading away down the slope. This pack was on the ground beside me, so I picked it up. And when I looked back, there was no door and no house, nothing but moorland and sky all around. So I started off along the track, because that was what she'd told me to do. And because sooner or later I knew they'd find a way to follow.'

He stopped. 'And here I am.' he said.

'Oh West,' Cally said in a whisper. 'That's terrible. That's –'

'Don't worry,' he said. 'It seems like a long time ago now. Yes, it was the most terrible thing in the world. But it happened. And all I can do now is what she told me to do. Look for my father. Go to sea.'

Cally said, 'How did she know about the door?'

Westerly shrugged. 'My mother's . . . different. Was different. She'd always known things. She taught me some of them – words, rhymes, things to do with my knife. Sometimes I'd walk into the room and she'd be talking to herself as if there were somebody else there. I was a bit scared of her, to tell you the truth. But she knew things. She even knew about you.'

'Me?'

He hesitated. 'About your hands.'

Cally's hands on her lap curled into fists, covering the deformed palms. Westerly reached over and took one hand, opening it gently to show the thick scaly skin. She made a face, pulling back, but he held on. He said; 'I didn't tell you the last thing my mother said. It was that I could trust three that I would meet. A man with eyes like an owl, a girl with selkie hands, and a creature in a high place.'

Cally looked at her hands. 'What's selkie mean?'

'I don't know,' Westerly said. 'But it has to mean you. I've already met the man with eyes like an owl. He's called Lugan.'

'Lugan's folk,' Cally said, remembering.

He looked at her quickly. 'Do you know him?'

'No. It was something someone said.' She thought of Stonecutter, and hoped he had not blamed Ryan for her escape when he woke.

Westerly drank from the flask, put it back in his pack and stood up – then leaned towards the window suddenly, staring down. 'God Almighty. *What's that?*'

Cally's heart jumped. She turned to look, but Westerly was fumbling with the catch of the window. As he pushed the broad iron frame open, she heard from outside a long

72

rumbling crashing roar that was in a moment dreadfully familiar.

She looked out, across the island treetops. On the far shore of the lake, like a great herd of elephants, grey formless shapes were welling out of the trees and down into the water. A faint sound of splintering came on the air, under the long rumble of stone against earth, and she saw trees quiver and fall, one after another, as the People ground them out of their way. Steadily the huge stone figures lurched forward, splashing into the lake, making straight for the island. As they disappeared under the water, others came moving after them, over them, moving into place until an edge of stone remained visible above the surface. Gradually, inexorably, like building-blocks moved by an invisible giant, they were making themselves into a causeway from the shore of the lake across to the island.

Cally felt sick with fright. 'It's the People,' she said hoarsely. 'Making a way for Stonecutter to come after me. I didn't think he would.'

Westerly pulled his head back in. He looked pale. 'What are those things?'

'Stone. People made of stone. Nothing but stone at night, but alive in the daytime.' She looked for the sun, but it stood too high to be seen from the window. 'And there's a lot of daylight left.'

'And Stonecutter?'

'A man. Sort of. He belongs to the Lady Taranis. He wanted to keep me for her.' Suddenly Cally panicked. 'We've got to get out of the tower, we've got to. We'll be trapped!'

She grabbed Westerly's arm; they snatched up their packs and hurried out of the room to the landing. But the white light was there facing them; not lying quiet in the stairwell now but boiling up in a whirling white cloud over their heads, forcing them back. It seemed alive, vicious

73

menacing: a column of boiling white gas driving them away from the stairs.

'Quick!' Westerly pulled her towards the other door, the dark entrance with its worn legend overhead: WESTERLY.

'But it won't let me in!'

'Yes it will.'

He pulled out his knife and held it before him towards the door, point outwards, like a threat. 'Open for Calliope,' he said.

And the door swung open, and Cally saw light inside, and Westerly drew her in.

Chapter IX

The ceiling and one wall were dark blue, and painted overhead were the bright patterned points of the stars, glittering; even through her daze of fear Cally could see Orion there, and Betelgeuse, and the clustering Pleiades. Hanging from the ceiling, as though it sailed through the painted sky, was a beautifully detailed model of a square-rigged ship.

She saw on one wall a huge picture of an empty desert, the sand sweeping and curving in long smooth dunes; around it were shelves filled with books and glass jars and chunks of many-coloured rock, strange intricate pieces of machinery, the brilliant blue wings of a bird spread and mounted, the white grinning skull of a horse. In one corner of the room stood a small neat bed; in another a big desk, set out with pads of writing-paper and a broad white sketch-book, and jars of pens and pencils and brushes. She saw an artist's easel, and a stand holding an enormous book open at a page of illuminated manuscript written in a language she did not understand. She thought: *this is Westerly; I don't know him —*

Westerly said abruptly, 'Check through the window. That one.' He jerked his head, bending over something beside the desk that she could not see.

Cally went to the tall window in the far wall and knelt on the window-seat, looking out. In the lake, the causeway had grown; steadily the massive forms of the People were lumbering along it, splashing into the water at the end, piling themselves in endless rows to form a path through the dark water. The closed window kept out the thunder of their moving, but she could feel a faint menacing vibration through her fingers on the sill.

On the far shore she saw the figure of a man, motionless, waiting.

She swung round. 'Stonecutter's there! They've almost made a way for him. What –'

Westerly was hauling on a vertical metal wheel as tall as himself; she was certain it had not been there before. He grinned at her. Pausing for breath, he said, 'There was always a trapdoor, in my dream –' and he hauled again at the wheel, and above their heads a section of the sky-painted ceiling swung down and a rope ladder fell into the room, dangling.

'Go on up,' Westerly said. He caught the ladder and held it taut. Nervously Cally took hold of the wooden rungs and began to climb, clutching tighter as the rope swayed.

Westerly called up after her, 'Keep your head down, or they'll see.'

Cally hauled herself out through the opening. The rough stone bit at her hands. She was out on the top of the tower, on a broad expanse of mortared stone; high crenellated walls stretched all around her in a square, their tops alternately as high as her waist and higher than her head. Clear blue sky filled the high world, and the sun was hot; from below came the grinding and thudding of the stone People at their dogged advance.

Westerly came up after her, coiling the rope ladder, shutting the trapdoor. 'Well, if no one can get into that room but me –'

The noise below suddenly stopped. They could hear nothing but the small whine of the wind round the walls. Looking down, pressed cautiously against the parapet, they saw Stonecutter crossing his living stone bridge to the island.

Westerly said, 'Does he want to take you back?'

'I think he just wants to stop me.' Cally felt cold at the thought. 'The woman he lives with – she gave me a message to carry. I think – he doesn't want the message to go.'

'Well.' Westerly said cheerfully, 'he's out of luck. We re on our way down from here.'

'How?'

'I'll show you.'

They saw Stonecutter look up at the tower. Striding towards it, he disappeared into the trees.

Westerly swung his pack down from his shoulder and began rummaging inside. But Cally grabbed his arm.

'Look at the People!'

They saw the waters of the lake swirl and the grey causeway begin to disappear, as the giant stone figures, dark and shining wet now, came crowding up out of the lake on to the island. Like a tide they came, steadily advancing; as they reached the edge of the trees they divided, and moved off in a grey line in either direction. The tower shook with their tramping. The People lumbered on.

Westerly frowned. 'What are they doing?'

'They'll make themselves into a wall, all round the island To keep us inside. I've seen it before. And unless we can get to that boat before they do –'

'Hum.' Westerly said. He went on searching inside his pack.

Cally looked up anxiously at the sun. It was scarcely past its peak; there were hours yet before it would go down, and not the smallest cloud hung in the sky to cut off the light that kept the People alive. Stonecutter had plenty of time to spare. Nothing moved in the sky but a small hawk, high up, drifting to and fro.

If you are in great trouble ever, Ryan had said, *call upon the birds of Rhiannon of the Roane.*

'Oh birds of Rhiannon,' Cally said miserably, half to herself, 'please come.'

Lazily the hawk drifted into a long curve. and flapped slowly away into the distance.

'What?' Westerly said, straightening up.

'Nothing.'

'Look.' He was holding out both hands to her. One held a small cloth bundle tied in knots at the top; the other hand was closed into a fist. 'One of these will help us. Either one. Choose.'

Cally hesitated, and pointed to the fist. Westerly put the bundle carefully back into his pack, then opened his closed hand. On the palm lay a carved wooden dragon, no more than three inches long. The sunlight glinted on two tiny red gems set in for its eyes.

Cally reached out a tentative finger. But before she could touch it, there was a crash behind them on the roof, and they swung round.

Stonecutter was standing there.

He was a towering dark figure against the sun-washed sky. They could not see his face. He said softly, 'Did you think you could keep me out? Did you think I had no power in this place? This is my tower, every stone of it. I built it for the Lady Taranis, long ago.' He kicked the trapdoor aside, and came towards them.

Cally shrank back to the wall. Westerly jumped in front of her, and his arm jerked sideways so that the tiny carving seemed to leap out of his hand and down to the stone floor at Stonecutter's feet. As it fell, in an instant too swift for their seeing the dragon was at once alive, growing, growing, filling the roof: a gleaming, sinuous winged body in loop after loop of armoured spiny scales. Clawed feet scraped needle-sharp against the stone; a magnificent huge-eyed head reared up, shining like bronze, agape with long glittering teeth. The winding body curved round Stonecutter; hissing, the dragon raised one sword-like talon to strike.

But Stonecutter laughed. Standing tall and unconcerned,

he stretched out his hand and touched the gold-brown scales – and instantly the dragon turned to stone. All colour went from it, all movement, all life; grey-white and silent, it stood forever motionless up on the roof of the tower, sightless eyes gazing through Stonecutter: a great stone gargoyle caught out of life as swiftly as it had grown.

Stonecutter stepped out of its coils, and advanced on them. His white face was tight now with rage, the dark eyes fixed and blazing.

'What did she give you?' he said. His gaze was on Cally: cold, malevolent. 'What did she tell you to take?'

'Nothing,' Cally said in a whisper.

He glared, unheeding. 'She gave you a message. No one shall take a message from Rhiannon. I took her, and I keep her for ever.' He was close now, reaching for her.

'Run!' Westerly said fiercely, pushing Cally aside, and gasping in terror she dodged away along the wall out of Stonecutter's reach. As the man swung round Westerly darted in front of him, holding up his pack like a shield, daring him like a matador; but the sweat was cold on his face at the thought of the man's stone touch. One hand, one finger on them, and they would both be dead as the dragon. He thought in panic: *what can I do?* – and in a chill desperate instant he thought of his knife. His fingers found it, in the sheath clipped to the side of his pack.

Stonecutter leapt sideways, up on to the dead coils of the dragon. Westerly caught a glimpse of Cally's terrified face beyond, her long hair blown sideways by the wind, and he was possessed by a ferocious protective fury he had never expected to feel again. He flung himself after Stonecutter, holding his knife. Stonecutter jumped down from the dragon, reaching for Cally.

Cally twisted away, but tripped as she turned and went sprawling on the stone floor. With a triumphant shout the big man lunged forward, grasping at her arm – and his chest was against the tip of the knife Westerly was holding in both his hands. Westerly shut his eyes for a moment, and pushed.

He felt the man's weight against the hilt of his knife; he heard a snarl of rage. He saw Stonecutter's face close to his own, furious – but there was no fear in it, or pain.

'Fool!' Stonecutter spat out at him. 'Taranis protects me!' – and he jerked himself violently backward from the knife Westerly still clutched. The blade emerged from his chest with no drop of blood, as if it had never pierced him. But in the same instant Stonecutter's face contorted suddenly, horribly. He screamed, flinging his arms wide – and Westerly saw that his backward lunge had impaled him from behind on the upraised sword-sharp claw of the dragon he had made stone.

Stonecutter shrieked, 'Taranis! My Lady!' The sound ended in a dreadful gurgle, and bright blood came out of his mouth.

And there was music in the wind, and a swirl of blue brighter than the sky and Taranis was there.

Westerly drew back. She stood shining and terrible, and her young-old face was even more beautiful than he had remembered. But she was facing Stonecutter with a cold implacable accusation in her eyes.

'Help – me!' Stonecutter gasped.

'No,' Taranis said. The small pitiless word made the hair prickle on Westerly's neck.

Stonecutter's voice was imploring, fading as he reached for breath. 'You said – while I served you – I couldn t die . . .'

'While you served me,' Taranis said. 'Yes. But who serves me, keeps my laws. You have broken them. Your death is of your making, Stonecutter. You came after this girl hoping, in your arrogance, to keep your precious Rhiannon for all time – but nothing is for all time. That is my law. You came here to take life – but only I may take life, in this my country So you forfeit me your own.'

Stonecutter's eyes were bright, staring; they flickered from Taranis to Westerly, and then past him. A grimace like a smile twisted his agonized face; he said, forcing the words out: 'And . . . one . . . other.' Then his head fell sideways, and the dead weight of his body pulled him down from the stone claw that had held him, and he fell to the ground. Westerly turned away from the terrible wound in his back, gagging.

He saw Cally, lying still. Stonecutter's last words echoed in his head, and a cold fear came with them. Slowly, he reached out and touched Cally's arm.

She was stone.

Westerly cried out, flinching back as if someone had struck him. He spun round beseechingly to Taranis. 'Please – please –'

She looked at him without expression. 'He touched her, she said.

Westerly said, frantic, 'But you can bring her back!'

Taranis said calmly, 'No. The power dies with him. He is dead.'

She stood beside the walled edge of the tower, her blue robe shifting in the wind. The sunlight glimmered in her white-blonde hair. She was looking at him closely now, holding his gaze. 'I had thought to have two of you with me,' she said, 'but one will do. This is a lonely country, Westerly, peopled by memories and shades. I starve for company. When travellers cross my borders, I do not like them to leave again. I chose that you should stay . . . So the rooms were made ready for you and the girl, in this tower of dreams – built for me by that cold fool there.' She poked an indifferent foot at Stonecutter's body.

Westerly winced. She looked at him in surprise. 'The sight is familiar enough in your world, surely? But if it troubles you . . .'

Casually she raised a hand towards the dead man and flicked one finger upward. Stonecutter rose to his feet as if pulled by an invisible string, and the bloody wound was gone from his back.

Westerly gasped.

'Oh,' she said lightly, 'that is not him. He is gone. Can you not tell?'

Stonecutter's face was blank, the eyes expressionless.

'Go on your way,' the Lady Taranis said to him. 'Take the boat that is at the bottom of the tower. It will not be needed now.' She smiled gaily at Westerly.

Silently Stonecutter disappeared into the tower, the way he had come.

Taranis said, still smiling. 'I will make you a bargain, Westerly. Your Cally may walk and talk again – if you stay here. Give up your quest. Stay with me.'

'No!' Westerly said. Then he paused. 'You mean you'd really bring her back? Or would she be like him – like a zombie?'

'Zombies are undemanding company,' Taranis said sweetly. 'And you will have the tower and the island, your own city with its own wall.' She glanced down over the edge of the tower at the still grey line of the People, then back at him. 'And I shall come and see you, and we shall play chess.'

Westerly said fiercely, 'No!'

Her smile faded. 'Very well then,' she said coldly. 'Leave your little stone friend, and leave my country – if you can.'

She turned away from him, and her blue robe swirled like the slant of a breaking wave, and she was gone.

Chapter X

Westerly stood alone on the top of the tower, under the empty sky. The wind whined softly round the stone turrets. Miserably he looked at the figure that had been Cally, but he could not make himself go near. The one touch of his hand on the cold stone of her arm had been so terrible that he could not bear the thought of feeling it again. There was a numbness in his throat, and his eyes prickled; he felt swallowed up by loneliness, and an overwhelming sense of loss.

He pushed his knife back into its sheath. Lying at the top of his pack was the cloth-wrapped bundle Lugan had given him. Westerly picked it up; there was no other way to try, now. He reached for the first knot in the cloth.

But a flicker of shadow fell on his hand for a moment, and then another, and through the breathing of the wind he heard another sound: a whirring, murmuring chorus that grew steadily louder. He looked up. Something was coming from the sky, dappling the sun; dazzled, he raised a hand to shelter his eyes. And he saw them, coming towards the tower from all directions, wheeling down out of the empty air, spiralling up from the trees: a great cloud of birds, of all sizes and shapes and kinds, approaching. They darted and fluttered and soared, calling to one another; he heard the bubbling song of skylarks, the plaintive cries of gulls, the harshness of crows, the honking of geese.

Wondering, he backed away and stayed very still beside the wall, watching. And the birds came to the tower in a vast wheeling horde, blotting out the sun, hovering over Cally, and each one plucked a feather from its own breast and released it into the air. Like a rainbow of snow the small soft feathers fluttered down, drifting on the breeze, and fell where Cally lay; more and more, as the thronging, chattering birds dived and made way for others and were gone. The cacophony of their calling was so loud Westerly could hardly bear it; he hunched his shoulders, sliding his hands up towards his ears.

Then at length the voices began to die, and the last fluttering forms were curving by his head – swallows, darting and faintly piping, and a slow-flapping pair of doves, their wisps of grey down floating to the lovely mound of feathers that showed where Cally lay. Last of all, a small hawk fell from the sky like a stone; hovered; dropped a soft brown feather and darted away.

Westerly thought sadly: *they're burying her.*

But there was a stirring beneath the mound. For a frozen moment he stared. Then he saw Cally sit up, blinking, shaking feathers out of her hair.

Westerly gaped at her, feeling a great grin begin to spread over his face. She scrambled to her feet, brushing at the soft fragments of down that fell away from her with every move, and she looked round in amazement. She saw Westerly. 'What *happened?*' she said.

Westerly crossed to her. He put his arms round her and hugged her very hard, dabbing an awkward kiss at her cheek as he let her go.

Cally turned very pink. 'What was that for?' she said, busily brushing away more feathers than were there.

Westerly said simply, 'I'm glad to see you.'

She glanced up at him – but then her eyes widened and her face changed, and he knew that she was looking past him at the stone dragon, remembering. She said, in panic, 'Stonecutter –'

'Gone. Don't worry – he's gone. The Lady Taranis came and . . . took him.' He flinched from the images that would come if he told her more. 'He can't hurt you now. He's gone.'

Cally stared at him. 'Taranis came?'

'He was telling the truth – she had this place built for us. This tower of dreams, she called it. She wants to keep us here. Forever. To be with her.'

Cally said fiercely, 'I'd rather be dead!'

'We'll get away,' Westerly said, with a confidence he did not feel.

'Quick then – now!' Cally's voice was tight with fear. She ran to the empty square hole in the stone floor, where the trapdoor had been. 'Has Stonecutter really gone?' Without waiting for an answer, she swung herself down over the edge of the gap and sat feeling with her feet for the ladder.

Westerly grabbed for their packs. 'Here – let me go first.'

'Why?' Cally said. She disappeared. Westerly opened his mouth, shut it again and followed her. Looking back as he climbed down into the tower, he saw the stone head of the dragon outlined against a reddening sky, snarling frozen into the sinking sun.

Cally led the way down the winding stone steps, without a glance back at the rooms that bore their names and offered all their hopes. The cold white light of the tower flowed quietly round their feet, docile now as it had been when they first climbed the stairs. Westerly reached an experimental hand down into the white mist; it moved elusively away from his fingers.

He said thoughtfully, 'Maybe it only does what Taranis wants. Why does she want it to help us now?'

Unheeding, Cally marched across the lofty rock-walled entrance chamber, towards the outer doors.

'Be careful,' Westerly said, suddenly full of unease.

Cally said confidently, 'They'll open.' She reached out a finger and touched one of the tall slate doors, and with a slow deep creaking it slid to one side. They blinked as the sun blazed into their eyes, a great orange ball sinking towards the treetops; for a moment they could see nothing else in the open doorway.

Then Cally let out a choked gasp and lunged for the door again, and against the glow of the sky Westerly saw, very close, towering over the doorway, the great grey figures of the People. They were massed outside in a vast crowd, blotting out the trees. He stared in horrified fascination at their huge half-made stone bodies; at the faces that could see and yet had only shallow sockets for eyes. Then the heavy door slid shut again, as Cally seized his arm and drew him back into the depths of the room.

'Well,' he said, 'we aren't going *that* way.'

'They're so close!' Cally was shaking. 'And so many of them, all outside – waiting . . .' She noticed suddenly that Westerly was carrying her pack, shook her head in apology and took it from him. 'After sunset we could go,' she said, pale but intent. 'Between sundown and sunup they turn to stone. They really do.'

Through the door, they could hear a low rumbling: deep formless voices murmuring together.

'Don't count on it,' Westerly said.

'But I've seen it. I climbed over them, just like over a wall. If we wait just half an hour . . .'

'But are *they* going to wait for that?'

They stood in the cold empty room, the white mist of light lying like a pool beside them. Westerly fidgeted with the strap of his pack, and went back to the stairway from which they had come. He looked down into the black well of the descending steps, the stair they had not taken. 'There's one other way we could try.'

'Down *there?*' Cally crossed to look.

'Why not?'

'Those stairs go underground – how could we possibly get out that way?'

86

'Don't know unless we try.

'I wish you'd wait.'

'I don't like waiting,' Westerly said. 'Why don't I just go and look?'

Cally hesitated. Then she said unhappily. 'Well – I'll come too. If the light goes with us.'

Westerly set his foot on the first step, and like a stream of quicksilver the light flowed in before him. He turned to grin at Cally, doggedly following him, and they went down the stone stairway with the white stream around their feet But it did not go far. Within ten steps they came to a flat wall of stone set across the stairway, with only a narrow gap at its base.

The stream of light paused, and eddied backwards.

'Well,' Westerly said cheerfully, 'that's a challenge if ever I saw one.' He contemplated the stone barrier for a moment, then sat down facing it and began to wriggle his way under it, feet first.

Cally said, 'That wall's there to keep people out.'

'So were the doors. No handles, remember?'

'This isn't a door.'

'Come on,' Westerly said impatiently.

'You aren't hearing me.'

'Yes I am. You're one of those people who don't walk on lawns if there's a notice saying Keep Off the Grass.'

Cally said with spirit, 'That's right.'

'I'm not.'

'*You're* one of those people who tramp your big feet all over the lawn and kill the new grass they're trying to grow.'

Westerly laughed. 'That's right.' He slid forward and disappeared under the rock wall. The light flurried like splashing water on the step he had left. Cally sighed, sat down and wriggled reluctantly feet first after him. They could just make out the shape of the steps continuing downward before them. But the light, their obedient white river. had not come through the gap with them.

Westerly peered back at it and whistled. 'Come on. boy.'

Nothing happened. Cally looked up through the gap and saw the white mist retreating back up the stairs.

'It's going away ' she said uneasily.

'You scared it.'

'Westerly, how can we go down a stone stairway in pitch darkness?' She tried to keep her voice from quavering. 'We could fall. There could be *anything* down there.'

Westerly said nothing, but his hand reached out and found hers, holding it firmly, and very slowly he drew her on down the steps.

Cally followed, filled with misgiving, trying to think only of the reassuring grip of his hand. Blackness was all around them: she stared into it, eyes wide. and saw only blank dark. It seemed to fill all the world, all her senses. Down they went, further and further. Uneasiness curled round her mind – and then suddenly there was no room for it, or for anything.

The dark exploded around them. Above their heads, somewhere, there came a dreadful roar as if the world were splitting apart; a long terrible thunder, bursting in great booming crashes that made them flinch down against the stairs. They felt the stone shaking beneath their feet, and heard rocks and stones rattling down the steps towards them. Together they waited, paralysed. caught in the fear of the tunneled stairway crashing down on to their heads.

After a long time, the uproar began to die away, and through the singing in their ears they could hear only an occasional muffled thud above. like the falling of a last loose stone. The air was filled with a strong smell of dust.

Cally felt a tug at her hand; Westerly was crawling back up the stairs. She went with him; nothing on earth could have induced her to let go of his hand. They could tell when they had reached the dividing wall only when their heads hit the stone. There was no glimmer of light above Reaching up her free hand to find the gap through which they had come, Cally could feel only solid irregular rock. and the dust in the air now was so thick that it made her choke.

Westerly said hoarsely. 'It's blocked for good – down again, quick.'

They slithered back down the stairway for more steps than she could count, until he paused.

Cally said shakily, 'The tower.'

'Yes. The People – just before the sun went down –

'We'd be dead if it weren't for you,' Cally said. 'Buried If you hadn't made me come down here.'

Westerly shifted his hand in hers; both were wet with sweat. 'Maybe we *are* buried,' he said.

'I don't care,' Cally said. 'From now on I'll walk on the grass, whatever the sign says.'

Westerly laughed weakly, and began feeling his way on down the steps in the darkness, leading her with him. They could hear nothing but the slow slither of their tentative feet reaching out. The air was cool; the smell of dust grew fainter. Westerly tried to convince himself that this must mean there was air coming into the tunnel from somewhere far ahead; that they must be walking to something more than a dead end.

'Listen!' Cally said, stopping him.

Very faintly, as if it were buried deep in the earth beneath them, they heard a slow muffled thumping, regular as breathing. As they listened, puzzled, the darkness began to give way, until they could see the dim outline of the walls on either side, glimmering with a faint luminosity of their own. Peering close, Westerly saw that there were tiny bright particles embedded all through the rock. They glowed more and more brightly as he watched, pulsating gently in time to the strange heartbeat sound. Cally rubbed her finger on the wall, and when she brought it away, the fingertip was faintly glowing.

Then she stood still, lifting her head. Over the distant thumping, she began to hear new sounds.

They were faint but all-pervading; they came into her mind like a dream, flowing in and out of one another, never definite. Music was there, but no clear voice or tune; she heard birds singing, the sounds of animals, a sighing that could have been the wind in the trees or the sound of the unknown sea. Then there were voices, murmuring, indistinct.

She clutched Westerly's arm, and knew that he could hear them too.

'What is it?' she whispered.

The wordless music drifted through the air, and with it muffled conversations they could not quite hear, broken often by laughter. Then for a moment two voices rose above the rest, though still faint and faraway: a man's voice and then a woman's.

'. . . *better keep out of the apple tree now – the blossom will be setting . . .*'

'. . . *would you mind if I went to see him on my own – would you mind . . .?*'

Westerly saw Cally stand rigid, straining to hear. But the voices drifted away into soft laughter and a contented murmuring again, and were lost.

He said, 'What's up?'

'That was my mother, and my father! I know it was – the last things they said before they left.' She stared wildly round at the dim-lit walls. 'What does it mean? Are they here?'

Without waiting for an answer she broke away from him, running to the turn in the path that lay ahead. Westerly went after her. And at the bend, light broke over them like a wave, and everything that had been in their minds was wiped away.

The tunnel was gone. They stood in an immense cavern filled with light and colour and sound. It stretched before them further than they could see; its vaulted roof was lost in a tangle of thick tree-roots which reached straight down, here and there, to become massive pillars disappearing into the earth. Waves of colour shifted and danced all around them, as if they stood inside a rainbow, and the music and voices that filled the chamber swamped their senses so that all thought was gone. Instead, memories flickered and flowed; they were caught into the past, into the echoes of joyous moments from all the years that they had lived.

They walked slowly forward into the great cave, each seeing particular images, hearing particular long-lost, long-loved sounds. Each of them was held in a long private happiness, seeing it mirrored in the other's face; it was as if they had both come home, to a security and reassurance they wanted never to leave. Westerly was a small boy, laughing at a magical game that his mother played for him in the patterning of three white bones; Cally was up in the apple tree, calling down to her father from the cradle of breathing leaves . . .

All the time, in the distance, the steady rhythmic thumping from beneath the cavern went on and on. Imperceptibly it was growing louder, but neither Westerly nor Cally could hear it; held deep in memory, they wandered smiling through the brightness, entranced. The throbbing grew, a deep insistent rhythm beating in the air – until at last the fierceness of it broke through Westerly's ears to his mind and abruptly he stopped, shouting aloud in pain, holding his head to keep the noise out.

But he could not keep it out; like huge heartbeats the relentless sound hammered at him. The dream had turned to a nightmare. Before him, he saw in terror the ground begin to quake and heave in the same rhythm; the earth rose up, swelling and crumbling, snapping the root pillars aside. And then something burst through the ground in a cloud of dust and exploding dirt, and the giant throbbing suddenly stopped and was overtaken by a roar of breaking rock. A chasm split open at Westerly's feet, and out of it rose the black curve of a monstrous sinewy body, the arching back of a gigantic snake.

Westerly croaked, 'Cally!' But she still walked on, oblivious, smiling, and he knew that she was lost as deep in her past happiness as he had been himself a moment before. He flung himself towards her, but it was too late. Rearing out of the splitting, widening cleft in the cavern floor, the body of the great black snake whirled out and looped itself round them, and swept them both down into the dark.

Chapter XI

The darkness was laughing at her, embracing her; a voice filled it. She heard release and freedom and gaiety, all in the voice that came from nowhere and yet was everywhere deep and easy and warm.

'Your time's your own,' said the voice. 'Your life's your own, not hers. Don't be afraid of her, don't be afraid of anything. Follow your own way and enjoy it – what can she do to you? Stone faces, for goodness' sake! Stone people! All those pretentious games! Just keep your toes clear of her clodhopping creatures, and go where you want to go. You'll like the sea. Remember the breathing of the poplar trees? It sounds like that, the sea, and it feels like this –'

The darkness rocked her, gently, rhythmically; swaying in its grasp she laughed aloud for pleasure.

Then somewhere she heard Westerly's voice, clear, wary, challenging. 'Who are you?'

The rhythm of her rocking was like music.

'I am Snake,' said the darkness. 'You know me well.'

Dreamily Cally sensed Westerly's resistance. He said again, 'Who are you?'

'Just now, my boy, I'm the saving of you,' the darkness said, with a touch of irritability. 'Time Present and Time Future, yanking you back out of the past. You really must watch for her little tricks. Voices, lights, music – if you let them suck you in, she has you. And you have to be rescued – if you're lucky – by Snake, grabbing you in that unceremonious way. Though I must say you did better than our Cally here.'

Cally remembered. It was like a discord in the music. 'But I heard my mother and father –'

'You heard nothing but memory,' said Snake sharply. 'You must go on, to the sea.'

'I heard them,' Cally said. 'They were *there*.'

'They are everywhere and nowhere,' Snake said. He was like a voice from a dream. 'They are not in the land of Taranis, not now.'

She said, 'You mean they're dead, don't you?'

The voice sighed, and the sigh ran through her with the rhythm of the rocking. 'Oh, selkie girl, selkie girl – wherever they are, they have not become nothing, they are not gone as if they had never been . . . Your world is all change, all journeying, and nothing that happens and no one that lives is ever lost. You above all should know that, Cally, selkie girl.'

There was a prickling in the palms of Cally's hands. 'What do you mean – "selkie girl"?'

'I will show you,' he said. The darkness whirled round her, and for a flash she saw his face, and it was the laughing bearded face of a man. Then it was gone, and she was lying on the air, turning, diving, and there was a blue-green light around her, misty and diffused, and she was not in air but in water. Cally who could not swim was swimming, delighting in speed, turning this way and that and up and down; no longer breathing, yet not conscious of holding her breath. She saw the deep sea below her, and in it a thousand schooling fish, all twisting in the same silver-flashing instant as if they were part of a single mind – and then breaking in a scatter of panic as sleek dark shapes dived down at them from above. She was swimming with her arms at her sides and her feet tight together, swimming with her turning body; she looked at the dark seals diving around her and knew that she was no longer Cally, but one of them. And between and among them all swept a long sinuous shape moving almost too fast to be seen, weaving and diving and doubling back on itself with all the joy of movement that Cally felt in herself. She heard his laughing and she knew that it was Snake, and knew too that she would never see him clearly; that he was not a separate being but a fierce distillation of feelings and powers that she had never yet properly known.

She rolled over in the still water and saw the bubbling flurry of the waves above her head; heard their hissing rhythm distant in her ears.

Snake said into her mind, 'Your oldest self is remembering – the part deep down that you cannot control, that comes from your ancestors who are forgotten. Even your mother had forgotten them, and her mother before her – no one had ever told them the truth. About the selkies, the seals who are human when they put aside their skins . . .'

Cally swam round and about him, feeling her strange-familiar skin, watching the sliding coils of the dark body that would never stay still.

Snake said, 'If a selkie should put aside her skin to swim as a girl, she is in danger. For a man may find it and take it, and then she cannot go back to the sea as a seal, but must follow him to beg for her skin. And if he hides it, she will have to live with him, marry him, bear his children, for as long as he keeps it hidden. She sings of the sea that she has lost, and her children and her children's children are born with webs between the fingers and toes, or a horniness of the skin of their hands, that goes on down the generations for ever. And always those of selkie blood dream of the sea, even if they have never seen it, and always the selkie-singing can fill them with the joy and the horror that their selkie ancestor felt on the day that she lost her skin.'

In the hissing of the waves Cally heard again in her memory the spectral singing that had been like her mother's voice and yet not like, and she remembered her own fear.

and the reaching out of her hands. 'So some great-great-great-grandmother of mine, a long time ago –'

'– belonged to the selkie folk,' said Snake, 'the folk that they call the Roane.'

Cally leapt through the water in a sudden flurry of understanding. 'Ryan! That's what he kept hidden – *that's* why her hands –'

'Rhiannon of the Roane,' Snake sang into her mind. 'Rhiannon of the Roane . . .'

The whirling and the darkness came again, and the itching in Cally's palms, and she knew as she rubbed them that she was herself again, back from the sea, suspended in the nothingness into which Snake had carried them at the first. She thought of Westerly and instantly saw him: standing straight-backed and alert, his chin up and his mouth a thin hard line, staring at something she could not see.

'West!' she said. 'What is it?'

Westerly seemed not to hear her. She said in alarm to Snake, 'What's wrong?'

'He holds to his nightmare,' said the deep voice all around her; there was compassion in it now instead of laughter. 'He has more of Snake in him than you do, he is all confidence and delight when he is fully awake. But he has a haunting, and he will not let it die, it pursues him . . .' He called out, 'Westerly! Let go! You have no right to guilt, your mother was killed – there was nothing you could have done –'

'I could have reached her sooner,' Westerly said, tense, miserable. 'I could have moved her out of the way.'

'Let go, Westerly.' Snake's voice was gentle. 'Taranis will do this to you if you let her, it is her nature. You mustn't let her. It is not your own mind you hear, it is Taranis – like the music of guilt and fear that sent Cally through the mirror. Westerly, listen to me. *It was not your doing. All living things die when it is their time. Let go!*'

Westerly said in anguish, 'I could have helped, I should

have helped. And they're coming – look, they're coming!'
His voice rose, high with dread, and Cally felt desperate for
him.

'Let me see,' she said urgently. 'Let me see what he's
seeing.'

'No,' Snake said. 'My business is to anchor you in life, not
to set you on a nightmare.'

But she could feel only the urge to share with Westerly.
'Please – let me see!'

'Very well,' Snake said, resigned – and the darkness round
Cally was all at once the darkness of a small child alone at
night in a big empty house, full of uncertainty and formless
fear. She too thought with terrible conviction, *they're coming,
they're coming*, and spun round nervously, hunting for
shapes in shadows. And then she saw them.

They moved only very slowly, but the sense of pursuit
was unbearable. She knew she was being followed, she knew
she must run for her life. She threw all her strength into the
effort to escape, and yet her body would not answer, but
moved with immense crawling weight. Frantic, flinging
herself forward, she crept like a snail. And they were gaining
on her: two huge looming figures, dark, faceless, reaching
out –

Cally shrieked. And at once Snake seized her back from
the black imagining and carried her away, so that it was all
gone from her mind as if she had never known it. He carried
her away into a rocking music with sunlight in it, and the
smell of lilacs, and the song of birds. New images wheeled
round her mind; through green branches and flying clouds
she saw a glimmer of Snake filling the world. It was the
Snake of the sea. She saw the lithe sinuous body carrying
her – and yet still within it the face of a man, laughing. The
face belonged to the voice that had enveloped them and
caught them back out of memory. For an infinite time he
sang to her, rejoiced with her, caressed her; across her

97

breasts and up through her body delight blazed like sudden fire, so that she felt herself wholly, fiercely in life in a way she had never known before. Her back arched with wonder, against a swaying floor, and she laughed aloud and opened her eyes to sunshine and a clear blue sky.

She was in a boat. Westerly lay motionless beside her, propped on one elbow, watching. His eyes were dark-shadowed with baffled excitement, and a wary, formless jealousy. He said huskily, 'What is it?'

Cally's smile was joyous, open. 'Snake –'

Westerly turned abruptly away from her into the stern; the boat swayed. Cally sat up, and gasped at the sight of the world around them.

They were drifting slowly down a river, in a broad, flat-bottomed boat, through a haze of green light. Meadows stretched away from the grassy banks on either side, edged with flowering hedges and trees; massive willows leaned over the banks, trailing their long slender leaves in the water. Sunlight glittered through the branches.

'It's beautiful!' Cally said. 'Where are we?'

Westerly said, not looking at her, 'How would I know? On a river, in a boat.'

She stretched happily, reaching her face up to the sunshine. 'Headed for the sea. Away from the tower, away from the People –'

'Without any oars.'

'Oh.' She looked round the boat vaguely. 'Well, who needs oars? The river's taking us.'

Westerly said stiffly, 'I'm sorry about your mother and father.'

Cally sat looking at the dark-green water moving past the sides of the boat. She said at last, 'I think I knew, really. They'd never have left me alone, otherwise. It's all right. Snake helped.'

'Yes,' Westerly said. He sat hunched in the stern of the boat, his arms round his knees. 'Yes.'

Cally said hesitantly, 'Have you ever –?'

'Ever what?'

'Nothing.' She picked a floating twig out of the water. 'I suppose he brought us here.'

'I suppose he did,' Westerly said.

Cally looked at him curiously. 'What's the matter, West?'

'Nothing,' he said coldly. 'Nothing at all. I just think it's pretty remarkable how you can find out in one moment that your parents are probably dead, and then in the next be all happy and smiling because of – Snake.'

'It wasn't a moment,' Cally said, wondering. 'It was a long time. And I think I'll see them again, somehow. He made me feel that. He took the pain away.'

Westerly made a small scornful sound like a laugh, un-smiling. 'He certainly did.'

'Westerly, what's the *matter* with you? Whatever Snake is, whoever he is, he saved us. He took us away from there. That's the only thing that's important.'

'Other things are important too,' Westerly said. He sat upright, his face enclosed, expressionless. 'Look, I think you'll do better if I'm not around. I don't feel like very good company at the moment. Snake seems to have made you feel you're on your way to the sea – I expect he'll make sure you get there. Maybe I'll see you then.'

Before she could say anything, he swung himself over the side of the boat and into the water. It was not deep; he found himself standing waist-deep, a few feet from the bank. The boat went shooting out into mid-stream, rocking wildly; he saw Cally clutch at the sides for balance. An eddy caught it there, and within seconds Cally was much further off, out in the middle of the river, drifting away.

He heard her call unhappily after him, but he turned his back and splashed up on to the bank. As he climbed out, trousers dripping, shoes squelching he found a figure standing close in front of him. He looked up. startled. It was Lugan

The lean, bright-eyed face was looking down at him without warmth 'That will make you feel no better. not at all.' Lugan said

Westerly said, 'I don't care.' Then he said, slowly, as if the words forced themselves out of him, 'Who is Snake?'

Lugan was peering after Cally; she was a small, hunched figure in the drifting boat. He began walking along the bank in the same direction as the river and the boat, motioning Westerly to follow.

'Snake,' he said, 'has much in common with the part of yourself that is giving you trouble at the moment.'

'I don't know what you mean.' Westerly said resentfully. His shoes sucked at his feet as he walked. He lengthened his stride to keep up with Lugan's long legs.

'Energy,' Lugan said. 'Enjoyment. delight, a glad fierceness. Snake is in a fever of living – like the young.'

'I don't trust him,' Westerly said.

Lugan said sharply, 'You share his preoccupations, you owe him your life, and you are jealous of a seeming reality you know nothing about. Stop it. And watch the river for your girl.'

'She's not my girl,' Westerly said, but he turned his head to the river. He had suddenly remembered that Cally could not swim.

They skirted a clump of willows, and when they were in sight of the water again he saw that it was running more rapidly now. The boat was swaying in the current; Cally sat tense and upright. Ahead, the river seemed to narrow; he saw pilings along the near bank, and immense wooden posts in the water, with what seemed to be a huge pair of gates holding the water back in a swirling pool. A small white-painted house stood on the bank beside the gates: a picture-book cottage, banked with roses and hollyhocks, and white clematis starring the walls around the door.

Lugan said in quick concern, 'The lock!' He began to run. Taken by surprise, Westerly pounded after him, down the rutted earthen path along the riverbank. They reached the cottage, and the first great pair of sluice-gates set into the water; Westerly saw that the lock was like a narrow enclosure with gates at each end, controlling the flow of the river. The first gates were closed, and there was a four-foot drop between the river and the level of the water enclosed inside.

Lugan began turning a metal crank set on a post beside the lock, and the waters of the upper river swirled as a sluice below the surface opened to let them pour through. He called over his shoulder, 'Watch Cally!'

Westerly was already waving at her from the bank. 'Don't stand up!' he yelled. 'Keep the boat balanced!' He glimpsed her face, wide-eyed and uncertain. 'Grab a branch if you can, but *don't stand up!*'

The boat brushed by the dropping fronds of a willow tree; Cally managed to grasp two of them, bracing her legs against the bottom of the boat so that it stayed there with her, turning, waiting. The river-level inside the lock rose and rose, as water poured in through the sluice; when it was the same as the level at which the boat lay, Lugan spun another crank and leaned his tall frame against a long heavy beam of wood, a great lever attached to the gates. Westerly ran to help him, and as they pushed the lock gates opened.

Lugan called, 'Cally! Let go! Let the boat come through!'

Westerly saw Cally hesitate as the unfamiliar deep voice rolled out to her over the water. He waved reassurance. Cally released the willow branches, and the current caught the boat and turned it towards the lock. She fended it off from the gates as it floated inside.

Westerly came to the edge, fumbling for words of apology.

but she grinned up at him. 'Neat. Like a staircase.' She pointed ahead to the further sluice-gates, beyond which the lower river now lay four feet below the water in the lock. 'Now you just let the water out till it's at that level, open the gates and out we go. Yes?'

Lugan was already leaning on the beam-lever to close the first sluice-gates again. 'Yes,' he said, smiling down at her; but then concern was back in his face. 'We must hurry. These locks were built not only to control the river – but to control those who go through.'

'This is Lugan,' Westerly said to Cally.

She sat very still, gazing up at the tall lean figure, the gold-brown hair. She said slowly, 'I've seen you before.'

'Yes,' Lugan said. 'When you were very young. Your mother was –' He stopped, his bony face suddenly secret and dour.

Cally said, 'One of Lugan's folk?' The words had come unbidden into her head; only as she heard them did she remember Stonecutter using them.

Lugan glanced at her quickly, but he said nothing. He turned toward the second sluice-gates, beckoning Westerly to come with him.

The door of the cottage opened, and the Lady Taranis came out.

For a moment there was silence, as they stood frozen, watching her. The hood of her blue cloak was down over her neck; her hair glimmered in a white halo. She said softly, looking at Cally, 'Any boat passing through my lock must pay a toll.'

Cally cleared her throat. 'What kind of toll?'

'A life,' Taranis said. Her voice was very sweet, and cold as snow.

Lugan said sharply, from the other end of the lock, 'That is not your law.'

'Sometimes I change my laws,' Taranis said.

He came towards her, towering, quiet. 'These two are not your people. They are not here as the others are. They are travellers, free to come and go. You may watch them, steal from them, go by their side, but you cannot keep them yet, if they wish to leave your land.'

Taranis' blue eyes blazed at him; she stood in an ominous stillness. Watching. Westerly and Cally hardly dared breathe.

'Do not cross me,' she said to Lugan softly.

'These two are my charge,' he said.

She took a deep breath, sweeping her cloak close round her, and shrieked at him, 'Then pay their toll!' She flung out one arm, pointing downstream at the river. The echo of her voice seemed to hang over the water in the still sunshine, and then gradually in the distance they heard a long low rumbling sound like a far-off train. It grew louder, approaching. All other sound had stopped; no birds sang.

Lugan swung round and reached a long swift arm down to Cally. 'Come up, girl.' He half-lifted her out of the boat, and she scrambled up on the bank. The roaring grew, and as they looked out down the river they saw in disbelief a huge wave rushing towards them, rearing up, more than a man's height.

Taranis began to laugh.

Lugan pulled Westerly's pack from his shoulder and thrust it into his hands. 'The knotted cloth I gave you, boy – quickly! Open it, and the winds will carry you.' He pushed them both towards the cottage. 'Against the wall – now!' His voice rose over the roar of the water. Westerly seized Cally's arm and they ran for the flower-bright wall.

'Why isn't he coming?' Cally looked back over her shoulder. Taranis stood staring triumphantly at Lugan, her laughter rising shrill through the tumult, and the wave rose green-brown towards them in the river. But it did not sweep straight on, over the banks and the two standing figures; it reared back at the first set of sluice-gates, pausing, enormous, and then curled down and wrapped its waters round Lugan as if it were alive, a huge grasping fist. Cally screamed. Lugan's tall figure was tossed up in the breaking waters like a tree-trunk; she heard him call to them once more as he disappeared, but could not make out the words.

'West –' She spun round to him, but he was not looking; he had the knotted cloth in his hands and was fumbling with it desperately. The wave curled sideways and reached toward them as he wrenched the cloth apart.

And every tree along the river was flung bending to the ground, and every bloom was ripped from the vines and plants round the house, as suddenly the air all around them roared louder than the waves, and a great wind seized Cally and West and carried them high into the air and away.

Chapter XII

They tossed and turned through the air, buffeted this way and that by the disputing winds. Whirling through a blur of time and place, they could see nothing, hear nothing but confusion and turbulence; each knew only that the other was there, somewhere close by. The winds howled and whined and fought, tumbling them through night and day, warmth and cold; the long thought-numbing journey seemed to have gone on for a hundred years. Then the sense of quarrel around them grew so fierce that in their whirling they felt a soundless report as if the air that carried them had somehow broken apart, and they felt themselves falling.

They lay on sand, in hot sunshine under a clear blue-white sky. Slowly Westerly sat up. All around them he could see nothing but the long curves of sand-dunes, white and dazzling. The sand under his fingers was so hot it almost burned the skin, and his clothes that had been soaked by the river-water were stiff and dry. Cally was sprawled beside him, blinking up at the sky; nearby, both their backpacks lay. There was no mark of any kind around them on the smooth sand.

Cally lay basking in the sunshine, feeling it warm her through. She said drowsily, 'D'you think this is where he wanted us to be?

'In a desert? It's a great place to find water to follow to the sea.'

She sat up, her mind suddenly clear, filled with the memory of the breaking wave. 'West – d'you think he's still alive?'

'Not if she had anything to do with it,' Westerly said bitterly. He got to his feet and picked up his pack, brushing off the sand. 'I don't know what I think any more. About anything. I think we just have to go on.'

Cally stood up. 'Which way?'

He looked at the sun. It stood high over their heads, blazing down: there was no way of telling east or west. 'I don't know.'

Shouldering her bag, Cally scrambled up the side of the tall dune before them, slithering as the sand gave way at each step. Westerly followed. From the top, they could see nothing but the next white dune, and the next, all around. But far away on two opposite sides of the horizon, like distant mirror-images of one another, there were the hazy outlines of two ranges of mountains.

'One of those,' Cally said.

'Can't tell which one's nearer.'

She pulled off her jacket and stuffed it into her bag. 'You choose.'

'*That* way.' Westerly said, pointing, trying to feel positive. 'And we should keep watching, to check we're going straight – we'll be out of sight of it half the time.'

They began trekking over the sand, sliding up and down the long shifting dunes; before long the unfamiliar slanting walk made a constant ache at the backs of their legs. They struggled on and on through the heat, through the silent barren slopes ruled by the sun. Cally rolled up the sleeves of her shirt; Westerly pulled his off altogether, knotting the arms round his neck so that the shirt hung down over his back.

'Turn your collar up,' he said. 'Keep the sun off the back of your neck.'

Cally felt oddly shy at the sudden sight of his muscled shoulders. She said, 'You've been in the sun already – you're so brown.'

Westerly laughed. 'That's not suntan, that's nature.'

'Oh,' said Cally in confusion. 'I'm sorry.'

'What for?'

'I don't know. Making personal remarks.'

'Nothing personal about skin. It's yours we have to watch. Lily-white northerners aren't made for this heat.' He looked more closely at her damp, flushed face. 'You all right?'

'Just thirsty.'

He swung down his pack and took out the battered leather flask. 'Here – have a swallow. We'll have to ration it. If the heat really gets to you, tell me and we'll rest.'

Cally gulped a mouthful of water, resisting a strong urge to empty the whole flask, and handed it back. They went on. There was no sound but the steady muffled squeak of their footsteps in the sand, and no sight of anything all round but the glaring sand and the empty sky. Cally walked with eyes half-closed against the fierce white light. Her head began to ache. From time to time Westerly paused on the peak of a dune, to check that they were still headed for the distant hills. Their hazy outline seemed to grow no closer: he wondered wildly if the mountains were retreating as they approached. At each pause he searched the horizon behind them carefully too, but no one was following. The desert was empty, unpeopled.

They walked for a long time, stopping occasionally for a mouthful of water. At last Cally paused on a ridge of sand, gazing despondently ahead. 'We don't seem to have gained an inch.'

'Optical illusion,' Westerly said heartily. 'They're a whole lot closer than they look.'

'Or maybe they're a mirage – looking close, but really hundreds of miles away.' She sat down on the sand. 'Westerly, I don't think I can walk any more.'

He squatted beside her. 'The sun's going down anyway.

We have to think about what the nights will be like. Aren't they cold, in deserts?'

'Don't know. I'm a lily-white northerner. I can't imagine ever being cool again.' Cally pulled the pack Ryan had given her from her shoulder and began to tug at the contents. 'D'you know, I've never properly looked in here yet?'

On her jacket, she set out a clean shirt, skirt, underwear, socks and a knitted shawl of some soft, filmy thread she could not identify. Then there was a bottle of water – she crowed, holding it up to Westerly – and three square paper-wrapped packets, with a note attached.

'These are for the times when there is no food,' said the note, in a delicate, spidery hand. 'A little goes a long way.'

Cally passed it to Westerly and opened one of the packets. Inside were half a dozen flat irregular cakes of a crumbly, dark substance bearing a vague resemblance to toast. She broke off a piece, tasted it, and handed another to Westerly.

He chewed pensively. 'It's good.'

'Whatever is it? Tastes like a sort of dry meat loaf.'

'Dry – that's the only problem. I reckon we've got water for about two days at the most. Including that bottle of yours. Where did you get all that stuff?'

'Ryan. The one I told you about, who lived with Stone-cutter.'

They were both silent for a while. The soundlessness of the dunes and the heat of the sun pressed in on them. Over the ridge on which they sat, the sun was gradually sinking, golden and huge. Cally put Ryan's food packages back in her pack. ' "A little goes a long way," ' she said with deliberate forced cheerfulness, quoting. 'It sounds just like Ryan.'

'Here's what I've got,' Westerly said. He took his pack, which was three times the size of Cally's; pulled out a tightly-folded blanket, spread it on the sand and put on it an array of objects that made her blink. There was his knife in its sheath; a bundle of some mysterious white fibrous material;

the flask of water; a plastic-wrapped package of matches; a pad of paper and two pencils; a small bag of salt; a bundle of clothes; three small shiny white sticks; a coil of rope; a tin cup; a tiny, chunky, three-sided bottle of green glass; a battered towel and, wrapped inside it, a comb, toothbrush and a bar of soap.

Cally said, 'All this was in the pack when you found it waiting for you?'

'Most of it.'

'They thought of everything. Can I borrow the comb?'

'Whoever they were,' Westerly said, handing it over.

'What's that white stuff?'

'Shredded wood. Kindling, for lighting fires.'

'And those white sticks?'

Westerly hesitated. He reached out a finger and touched one of them gently. Then he said, almost reluctantly, 'They weren't in the pack. I had them in my pocket. My mother gave me them once. They aren't sticks, they're . . . bones.'

'Oh,' Cally said blankly. Something told her to move on to the next thing. 'What's the little bottle?'

'I don't know.' Westerly picked it up, opened it, smelled it, made a face. Cally took it from him and sniffed.

'Bluuucchh,' she said.

'Must be some kind of medicine. Nothing else could smell so bad.'

'I wonder what it's for?'

'I dare say we shall find out.' Westerly put down the bottle and pulled what looked like a roll of shiny cloth from the bottom of his pack. 'This is the last thing.'

She watched as he unrolled it. Wrapped inside was a bundle of thin metal rods. Westerly began fitting them together into the outline of a small pyramid, and suddenly she realized what he was doing.

'It's a tent!'

'Just about hold both of us, if you keep your elbows in.'

She helped him pull the thin, tough covering over the frame. The light was fading fast as the giant red sun sank beneath the horizon, and she was all at once desperately tired. The air was cooler now. They sat for a while as the outline of the dunes grew dim, and the stars pricked blazing pinpoints through the darkening sky; they ate another piece of Ryan's food each, and drank a mouthful of water, and then they curled up back to back in the tent. Westerly offered Cally his blanket, but she wrapped herself in Ryan's shawl instead and found it astonishingly warm.

Westerly lay carefully motionless, listening to Cally's regular breathing, very conscious of the curve of her back against his own. The stars flamed at him through the open flap of the tent; he recognized the Plough, high up, and gently raising his head he followed the line of the two marker stars until he could see the North Star. From where he lay, it hung to the right of the nearest tent-pole. He lowered his head again. With that and the sun, they could check the direction of their travelling tomorrow.

He was almost asleep when he heard, far-off out in the night, a high plaintive call, like a voice singing a single note. He felt Cally jump out of sleep; she propped herself on one elbow, tense, listening.

'What's that?'

The sound came again, more faintly: a sad, desolate call, like a creature lost in the night, calling out for an answer and finding none.

'Some night bird,' Westerly said. 'Don't worry. It's a good sign – means the desert must end somewhere. Good-night.'

She lay back again, relaxing into sleep. 'Night, West.'

Cautiously he reached out one hand to his pack. The knife lay there safe and ready in its sheath, comforting, waiting.

*

For two days they walked through the desert, knowing now that the mountains to which they were heading lay in the west. They started each morning at first light, while the air was still cool; but very soon each day after the sun burst over the horizon the heat grew fierce, beating the energy out of them. The sun burned their skin, so that even Westerly rapidly learned to keep his shirt on his back and his sleeves pulled down. Like a mirror the gleaming white sand threw heat up at them from below, and the air seemed hot and thick, difficult to breathe. In the hottest hours of the day when the sun was high overhead they gave up trying to walk at all, and crouched exhausted in the shade of the little tent, trying to forget their thirst.

They had nothing to eat but Ryan's food, and they ate little of that because it was so dry, but it seemed to sustain them. Their greatest worry was water. Though they drank only a little each day, Westerly's flask was empty and the bottle in Cally's pack now only half-full.

'I wish I was a camel,' Cally said.

Westerly said, 'I wouldn't want to spend this much time with a girl who looked like a camel.'

She tried to laugh, but her tongue felt thick in her mouth, and her mind full of hopelessness. 'When this is gone, we shall just die of thirst.'

'We'll be out of the dunes by then,' Westerly said encouragingly. But he knew that the mountains, though nearer now on the hazy horizon, were far more than a day's walk away.

On the second night, he had heard the strange plaintive cry again. It had called several times, seeming to come nearer, but then on a last bubbling, chirruping note it had died away. He wondered what bird could be calling so; he longed to believe that it belonged to a more hospitable place not far off, beyond the sand. He tried to put out of his mind the thought that someone was following them.

'You should call your birds again,' he said to Cally the next day.

She shook her head sadly. 'They couldn't come here. They'd all die.'

'I suppose so.' Westerly plodded on up the side of a dune, pausing at the top to stare out once more at the mountains. They seldom found a dune tall enough to provide a lookout, and often when they did find a sight of the hilly horizon again, they found they had curved round unknowingly and had been walking in quite the wrong direction. He wondered how many miles they were forced to waste in a day. Watching him, Cally studied his thin. sunburned face and tousled hair, and tried not to imagine what she must look like herself. They were both much weaker, and growing more tired all the time.

It was her turn to lie awake that night. looking at the thin new moon which hung overhead silvering the sand. They had only a few swallows of water left in the bottle; not even enough for the next day. What would happen then?

All around her in the huge sky the stars burned, myriad and distant; fewer, now that the moon was up, but still filling the sky. In her old life. she had never seen so many stars. Had her parents ever seen them, out in the night away from houses and cities? Could they see them now?

She closed her eyes against the sky. She and Westerly had begun sleeping in the open, using the tent as a groundsheet, glad of the cooler air. The nights were friendlier; it was easier to breathe. Cally lay relaxed, drifting into sleep.

The touch that brought her awake again was so soft that at first she did not open her eyes. Had she dreamed it, that gentle feathery brushing against her cheek? No – it came again, this time a soft tickling on her forehead. Drowsily she opened her eyes – and outlined against the bright sky, dark and angular and menacing, she saw a huge monstrous insect standing over her: a creature out of nightmare.

Cally shrieked, and rolled sideways, clutching for Westerly. The great insect leapt away. Westerly surfaced out of deep sleep. bemused by Cally's terrified grasp on his arm. 'That thing –' she was gasping. 'That *thing* –' Hastily he reached for his knife and scrambled up, looking round.

'What's wrong?'

'It was awful!' She stumbled nervously to her feet, staying close to him. 'Awful. Right next to me, touching me. A thing – like a mosquito three feet high.'

The sand lay silent and silver, filled with dune-shadows from the moonlight; the vast sky glimmered at them. There was nothing: no movement, no sound.

Westerly said doubtfully, 'Are you sure you weren't dreaming?'

Before Cally could answer, a voice came.

Chapter XIII

It was a small sweet voice like singing; it flowed into their hearing so gently that they were not sure if it touched their ears or their minds.

'She was not dreaming,' it said. 'I am here. I have been looking for you.'

Westerly could feel Cally trembling. He swallowed, and held his knife tightly. 'Where are you?' he said.

'You must not be frightened,' said the sweet-singing voice. 'I do not look – like you. You must not be frightened.'

To Westerly's astonishment, Cally said shakily into the darkness, 'I'm not frightened. Truly.'

Westerly peered all round at the quiet silver-lit dunes. 'Can you see me?'

'Of course.' said the voice, and there was laughter in it.

'Tell me where you are.'

The voice said, 'I am to your right, and a little ahead of you. In the shadow.'

'Stay there.' Westerly said. He stared hard into the moon-shadows of the dunes at the right of him, but could see nothing but bright sand and dark. Crouching, his eyes still on the sand, he groped behind him for his pack and felt about inside it. He found what he was looking for.

'What are you doing?' Cally whispered. She saw his hand holding three short sticks; then realized that they were not sticks, but the things he had called bones.

Still crouching, Westerly turned and set the three white bones on the sand in the shape of an arrow-head, pointing at the place from which the voice came. He touched each of

114

them gently with the point of his knife. Straightening up, he said softly to Cally, 'If they shine, it's good. If they stay dark, it – isn't.'

Cally stared at the three bones; she could only just see them, by the faint moon-shadows they cast on the sand. As she watched, they began to glow with a faint greenish light, brighter and brighter, until they lay flaring like cold fire.

The singing voice bubbled out in a long wordless sound of delight, and out of the shadows towards the three still flames, a creature came running. Westerly stiffened, and heard Cally gasp. It was not an insect, it was like nothing he had ever seen. It stood about half his height, and it was all thin lines, with no substance to it; there were six thin jointed legs, long and slender, and a small thin body and long neck, ending in a head so small it scarcely seemed to exist. From the little head four antennae waved: two of them were straight, with blunt ends that he supposed were eyes; the others were hair-like, flickering, constantly moving, stroking the three bright bones now in a kind of glad caressing.

The eye-stalks swivelled towards Westerly; the voice said happily, 'You have them from your mother then – Lugan's guardians. You are privileged.'

Cally took a deep breath and knelt down, squatting on her heels, her hands resting on her lap. 'He's Westerly,' she said. 'I'm Cally.'

The creature came towards her and paused a yard away. Cally stayed very still. There was a moment's pause, in the silent dunes. Then the creature came close to her, and its feathery antennae reached out and gently stroked her cheek. It was the same light touch that had wakened her.

'I am sorry I startled you,' the soft voice said. 'I have been looking for you. I am Peth. A . . . thing, as you said. A thing of the desert.'

'I'm sorry,' Cally said. 'It was just –'

'Never mind, never mind,' Peth said consolingly, as if to a

115

child. 'Come now, you should be travelling. There is not much time. Come with me.'

'In the dark?' Westerly said.

'The night is the time for travelling, in this land,' Peth said. The music of his voice was a reassurance; every time he spoke they seemed to feel strength flowing back into them. Cally looked at Westerly. In silence he put away his knife and bent to fold up the cloth of the tent. Cally helped him put it away in his pack.

They turned to Peth, and heard a soft, lilting sound, a sweet crooning. He was standing over the three glowing signs of the arrow, stroking them with his antennae, singing to them. His eye-stalks swung round to Westerly and Cally, and the crooning died away and the light went out of the white bones.

'Put them away now,' he said. 'Now I have spoken to them. It has been a long time. They will do more for you yet than perhaps you knew they could.'

Westerly looked at him warily for a moment, but said nothing. He put the three bones back in his pack.

They set off, following Peth. His insubstantial stick-like body was hard to see in the dim moonlight, and at first he flickered over the sand so fast that they lost him completely, and had to stop and wait. He came back, making small consoling sounds of apology, and afterwards stayed deliberately close to them, stepping delicately over the sand a few yards ahead. Cally could see flat pad-like feet at the ends of his spidery legs, keeping him from sinking into the sand.

Westerly paused. He was looking up at the sky. 'Peth.'

'Yes?'

'Cally and I have been trying to go westward.'

'To the mountains. Yes,' Peth said.

'But you're taking us south. I can tell by the stars.'

'Have faith,' Peth said. His delicate insect-like body moved ahead again.

'Hum,' said Westerly. He plodded on up the side of a dune, slithering under the weight of his pack.

Cally said softly, over his shoulder, 'I like him.'

'You like everybody,' Westerly said wearily

'I suppose you mean Snake.'

'It doesn't matter.'

'Your bone-things glowed for Peth.'

'I'm not arguing,' he said. 'I just like to know where I'm going.'

The moon was gone; the sky was beginning to grow light. Gradually the stars disappeared, and a cold greyness was everywhere. Without shadows, the dunes merged into an endless colourless world of dull sand.

Cally said, 'The dunes aren't so high here.'

'It's just the light,' Westerly said. He walked morosely on, following the high-stepping figure ahead; in the cool dawn Peth looked skeletal, macabre.

After a while he said, 'You're right. They're changing.'

Above them Peth paused on a ridge of sand, his body outlined spider-like against the brightening sky. They climbed towards him, and as they drew level the first rays of the sun spurted into the sky at their right hand, and before them they saw the end of the dunes, and the beginning of a new desert, vast and intimidating.

There was no sign of life or water or any green thing, anywhere. They saw that they stood in a huge valley, filled with rock and grey scrub, with mountains rising dark and forbidding at either side. The sun rose; their shadows lay long and thin on the last few yards of white sand.

Peth said, 'This is why I had to bring you south – to reach the solid land. Across the scrub, you will be able to reach the mountains before the sun dries you into dust – across the sand, you would have had no chance. In all that half of the valley the White Sea stretches right to the foot of the hills.'

'The White Sea?' Cally said.

'He means the sand,' said Westerly.

'The sand and the salt ' Peth said. 'If you had gone north, you would have come out of the dunes into a place still more deadly, a hard white land where the earth is paved with salt. A long time ago this valley was truly a sea, until the Lady Taranis took it. Now the water is gone, and only the salt and the sand are left.'

Westerly said bitterly, 'She kills everything.'

'Of course,' Peth said.

He ran down from the dunes to the stony land ahead; small eddies of dust stirred round his moving feet. Then he turned away towards the mountains, and they followed. They were travelling westward again, the sun hot on their backs. Wearily they trudged over the dusty rock-hard land, through grey scrub and shrivelled plants that looked as if they had never been alive. Sharp stones bruised their feet through the soles of their shoes; dust roughened their dry throats. All at once Cally felt giddy with heat and weakness. Her knees buckled; she crouched on the ground, head down.

Westerly called sharply, 'Peth!'

Peth turned. His spidery body glittered now in the sunlight, iridescent, shot through with shifting colours that never became distinct.

'We can't go on much longer.' Westerly's voice was hoarse. He looked down in concern at Cally. 'Where's that bottle? You need a drink of water.'

In relief she pulled it out of her bag and took a careful swallow, licking the last drops off her dry lips; then she held out the bottle to Westerly. He shook his head.

'Come on, West,' she said. Her voice sounded strange in her ears: husky and thin. 'Share.'

'Share,' Peth said. 'There will be water before nightfall.'

Westerly said bleakly, 'That may be too late.' But he

swallowed a mouthful of water. There was an inch or two left in the bottle. He corked it again, paused, looked at Peth. Slowly. as if forcing his own hand, he held out the bottle to him.

Peth made a rippling sound like laughter. 'Well done. But I do not need it. Thank you.' He turned in a slow semicircle, head up, eye-stalks and antennae stretched out as if searching. 'You must travel further. Slowly. easily. But you must come.'

Cally put the bottle back in her pack and stood up, unsteadily. Westerly reached to carry her bag for her, but she pushed his hand gently aside. Then she stiffened, looking out across the huge valley, squinting eastward into the sun. What's that?'

'Where?'

She pointed. 'There. Something moving.'

Far off, a plume of dust drifted up from the desolate grey land. Westerly stared, his eyes searching round the valley. 'There's another to the south. Look – there –'

Behind them, coming from the further range of hills, the two smoky tufts rose into the air.

'Fire?' said Cally.

'Dust,' Peth said, his soft voice sharper. 'The dust of feet, or of wheels. They have found you. Come quickly now, as quick as you can. There is not much time.'

They stumbled after his glittering, flickering shape with panic driving them. The wiry undergrowth caught at their feet; the twigs of small skeleton trees scraped their legs and arms. Westerly's mind was full of the nightmare images of his pursuers: *they're coming – I always knew they were coming* . . . Cally was trying to force out the memory of her terror-stricken flight from the People, and their crashing implacable progress through the wood. She said, hurrying, gasping, 'We stir up dust too – they can see us wherever we go.'

Westerly came close to her; he said, low and anxious,

'Maybe it's a trap – maybe that's why he led us out of the dunes. Got us out in the open, for *them*.'

'No!' Cally said. 'No!' She looked ahead for Peth, and saw him darting between branches as thin and angular as himself – and then suddenly he was gone.

'West! Where is he?'

Westerly said furiously, 'I knew it!' He swung round, staring back across the valley; the approaching plumes of dust were closer now, converging on them, and there was a faint humming sound in the air.

'What can we do?'

'Nothing. Run. Give me your pack.'

But from somewhere near their feet they heard the singing note of Peth's voice, calling to them.

'Cally! Westerly! Quickly – get down on your hands and knees. And look, and come forward.'

Westerly paused, suspicious, and Cally pulled him down to the ground. He turned on her angrily – but then amongst the thorny, clutching shrubs they could see Peth again. Unfolding his spindly legs, he was climbing out from beneath a shimmering, translucent covering woven between the lowest branches of a low dead bush. Cally saw that at the edges the covering was woven down to the ground too, leaving a space within it like an open-ended box. From above, it had been invisible.

'Inside!' Peth said curtly. 'Both of you. And whatever you may see or hear, lie still and silent, and wait.'

They wriggled into the tiny shelter and sat there crouched on the stony ground, in a haze of diffused white light that had in it none of the fierce heat of the sun. Even the blazing sunlight at the entrance seemed to be growing gentler too; peering out, Cally saw Peth's frail body flickering to and fro there so fast that he was no more than a blur of movement. Like a spider, he was weaving more of the strange shimmering web to cover them and hide them – but weaving far more than was needed just to cover the entrance. To and fro he flashed, back and forth, out on either side beyond the little shelter. He was making an invisible fence: a barrier. But what defence could it possibly be against the attackers rushing on them across the valley?

She reached out a tentative finger to touch the filmy covering round them, remembering the fragility of spiders' webs. But for the second her finger brushed the tiny filament, the air all around them seemed to fill with a sudden blinding light, and Cally was flung half-stunned against Westerly.

Peth's voice sang sharply from outside. 'Do not touch – *do not touch!*'

The humming from across the valley was growing louder, more distinct. Westerly had his head up, listening. His eyes searched anxiously for a gap anywhere in the luminous screen around them – and then he saw a slit of brighter light, and leaned eagerly forward, taking care not to touch.

He saw a great cloud of dust over the scrubland, coming close. Dimly inside it he could see two gigantic formless shapes, dark and menacing. Fear washed over him, and he gazed horrified, motionless, as they rushed headlong towards him. They were caught, he and Cally, trapped; in an instant they would be obliterated. There was no escape. He could hear a strange high sound from Peth, a high triumphant singing. He felt the weight of Cally's inert body against his side, and knew he should help her, yet still he could not take his eyes off the whirling dust outside, the growing, darkening cloud. The deep ominous humming filled the air, the huge pursuing figures loomed over him, so close that he could see their faces now – and he gasped in pure terror, for the faces, staring at him, laughing a dreadful cold laughter, were Cally's and his own.

He crouched, clenching his fists, waiting for them to break through the tenuous barrier of Peth's web as they rushed at it. And then, in an instant, they were gone.

Westerly stared. There had been no moment in which he saw them disappear. There was simply silence, nothing, no sign of any pursuit but the long lingering cloud of dust, drifting through the air.

He reached down to Cally. She lay still; her face was dry and hot, and her breathing shallow.

The filmy curtain in front of him split suddenly in two, and Peth was there, outlined monstrous against the unlit sky, laughing.

Westerly looked at him out of a blur of gratitude for which he could find no words. He said, 'What did you do?'

Peth laughed again. 'Your shadows are gone. They will not come back. When the nightmare cannot leap a fence, it loses all power. Remember that, Westerly-bound.' His eyestalks bent towards Cally. He said soberly, 'She is not well.'

'She needs water.' Westerly's voice was thick; his tongue felt huge in his mouth. He took the last of the water from Cally's pack, propped up her head and gently forced the rim of the bottle into her mouth. The water trickled through her lips; in reflex, she swallowed. Her eyes flickered open, and tried to focus. 'So . . . hot,' she said.

'Not for long,' Peth said gently. His long questing antennae reached forward and brushed Westerly's hand and wrist. 'Westerly, take Lugan's guardians from your pack and bring them out here to me.' He backed away, and disappeared outside.

Westerly took out the three white bones. Cally stirred, blinking, whispering. He bent his head to her.

'West – the chasing . . . what –'

'They've gone,' he said. 'Peth – killed them. You just rest.'

Her eyes closed again.

Peth was standing outside on the dry earth, among broken bushes and tumbleweeds. He made a soft, purring sound of welcome as he saw the three bones. 'What did your mother tell you about them?' he said.

122

She didn't tell me much.'

'She would have told you all she knew.'

Westerly's throat felt empty as he remembered his mother's face: the smile of pleasure in sharing, the conspiratorial delight in the dancing eyes as she had made him hold the bones, whispering to him. He had thought she was crazy, then.

He said huskily, 'She said, keep them always, they are very old and very powerful. If you touch them with your knife, they will talk to you, they will glow for safety and grow cold for danger. They will always be right. Trust them.' He looked up penitently at Peth. 'But I didn't trust you for a while, even though they told me to. I'm sorry, Peth.'

'You are learning,' Peth said mildly. 'That is what this journey of yours is for. And now you will learn something your mother did not know. Take the three and plant them in the ground, in a triangle. They must point upwards.'

Westerly did his best to drive the bones into the hard ground. They leaned sideways, and would not stand upright. He collected small stones and built a miniature cairn round each one, propping them so that they pointed to the sky.

'Good,' Peth said. 'Now listen well, and always remember. There is a calling you may do, for the sun, or the rain, or the wind. When the guardians are pointed to the sky, you must say the words . . .'

He lifted his head.

> 'Water and fire and air, by these we live,
> By rain and sun and wind.
> Oh sky I am in need.
> Send me the rain.'

He paused. 'Remember most of all that the need must always be real,' he said. 'Now – do you have it?'

123

Westerly nodded, intent. Taking a deep breath, he said clearly and slowly,

> *'Water and fire and air, by these we live.*
> *By rain and sun and wind.*
> *Oh sky, I am in need.*
> *Send me the rain.'*

Peth said, 'Each of us can do more than he knows. It takes only the teaching. Now – watch the sky.'

At first Westerly saw nothing but the hazy blue all around, and the glare of the sun. Then he realized that in the sky over the distant mountains a long low bank of cloud was growing. Slowly it rose and came towards them, grey-white and swirling; soon it filled half the sky, and still it came. It swallowed the sun, and the fierce heat died from the air. High up, racing on a wind he could not feel, the cloudbank swept across the valley to fill the whole sky. As it passed overhead, he felt the first few fat drops of rain.

Westerly whooped with delight, and turned his face upward. 'Cally!' he called. 'Cally!' He dived into the shelter and pulled her out. The rain grew heavier: they reached to it, opened their mouths to it, laughing in relief.

Peth laughed too. 'But stay inside,' he said. 'Wet clothes will not dry at night. See where the water comes to you.'

He waved his antennae at the strange translucent roof of their shelter, and although they could not see its substance they could see the water gathering in it, and spilling over one slanting edge. Cally set her mouth to the overspill; Westerly went burrowing for cup and flask.

They drank and ate and slept, while the rain pummelled at the roof and Peth stood watch outside. He made no move for shelter, but stood there with his antennae spread as if he were revelling in the rain. Glancing out sleepily, Westerly thought: *he's the colour of rain.*

When Peth roused them, the sky was clear and the moon

was high, and the travelling began again. They moved far more quickly now over the firm ground. and the mountains began to loom close and dark over the desert

And when the sun rose, and colour came back into the world, they saw that the rain had worked a transformation The desert was flowering.

All over the stony ground the leaves of small plants were fat and green, wonderfully restored from the grey tatters that before had lain limp and apparently dead. Each plant was starred with blossoms, white and yellow and red: white-budded sprays had sprung out of flat leafy rosettes scarcely visible before. Small round cactuses each wore a bright pink flower perched above their bristling spines. and in the tall spindly tree-cactuses, yellow and white blossoms hung in echo of the sun and moon. Everywhere. the grey scrubby ground was hazed with a faint mist of green.

Peth made a chirruping sound of pleasure and began bending his head close to the larger flowers, uncoiling a delicate proboscis that they had not noticed before, and drinking the nectar. He looked up at them, and waved his antennae at the white buds spraying out above his head. 'Those are for you.'

'To *eat?*' Cally said doubtfully.

Peth chirruped again, laughing. Westerly reached out tentatively and picked a bud; nibbled, then eagerly pushed it into his mouth and grasped for a handful. 'Mmmm.' he said indistinctly.

Cally picked one of the tight-closed white flowers and began dubiously chewing; then her face changed. 'Peaches.' she said, reaching for more. 'And oranges.'

'And pears and bananas,' said Westerly with relish. 'And I think just a hint of celery.'

'*Celery?*'

'Well, it's a nice change from dried meat loaf.'

They moved slowly through the scrubland. browsing like

contented cattle. Even Peth seemed quite lacking in any sense of urgency now. The sun rose higher, as hot as it had been before and yet no longer threatening.

'Peth,' Westerly said, 'what is this place?'

'The Valley of the White Sea,' said the soft singing voice.

'Have you always been here? How do you live?'

'No place is totally dead,' Peth said. 'Sooner or later the rains come. One needs only patience.' He bent his head, and uncoiled the long slender tube of his mouth into a flower.

Cally said, 'Are there others like you?'

'Not altogether like.' Peth stood still in the sunshine, his skeleton body gleaming; he looked like some great prehistoric insect, the last of a species vanished for thousands of years. He said, 'But Lugan's folk are everywhere. No one of us is like another. Even you two are not like one another.'

'Us?'

'Of course. You are in life – strongly in life, because you are young. So of course you are Lugan's folk.' His spindly legs tensed, and he turned away. 'Come – a little further, and then we must rest. And then travel again.'

Cally tried to keep his attention. 'Who is Lugan? Has Taranis killed him?'

Peth made a strange unnerving hissing sound; it was not anger or displeasure, but a kind of discomfort. 'Can the night kill the day? Can the winter kill the spring?' He made the hissing sound again, and strode off rapidly through the flowering scrub.

Chapter XIV

By the time they had reached the edge of the mountains, the flowers in the desert were dying, and the leaves shrivelling. The sun's ferocity was master once more; they could feel it drawing out their own vitality just as it drew out all moisture from the things that grew. But they had water with them, and Ryan's oddly invigorating food, and a store of the astonishing white flower-buds which Peth had made them gather and put away in their packs. For him, Cally carefully picked a supply of the long-throated flowers from which they had seen him feed.

Peth bubbled at her with a laugh that had affection in it, but sadness too. 'They will not live,' he said.

'Well, just for a while – won't they? Are we going far?'

The voice was totally sober for a moment. 'Very far.'

Cally said nothing, but wrapped the flowers carefully in Ryan's shawl and packed them away.

The mountains towered over them, bleak and intimidating. They began as brown foot-hills of dry clay, fissured and ridged so that it seemed impossible there should be a way up through them anywhere. Above, the peaks rose: hard grey rock, in crags and ravines reaching up out of sight into the sky.

They stood at the base, looking up. It was afternoon; the hot sun beat at them as if in triumph.

Westerly found himself feeling very small. He said, 'Is there really a way up there?'

'Just one,' Peth said. 'And I shall show you it. But it will be hard – harder than anything you have encountered yet in this hard land.' He was quiet for a moment, eye-stalks and antennae still, facing them. He said, 'Where are you going?'

'You know so much,' Cally said in surprise, 'you must know that.'

'Yes. But I want to hear.'

'To the sea,' she said.

'Westerly?'

'Yes,' Westerly said. 'Over the mountains to the sea.
Peth said, 'It matters?'

'It matters more than anything,' Cally said at once. Then she paused. 'I don't think either of us really knows why.'

'I do,' Westerly said belligerently. 'My father's there. And maybe yours too, and your mother.'

She looked at him, expressionless.

'Well,' he said more slowly, 'all right, no, we don't know for sure. But we do know it matters.'

'Keep that in your minds,' Peth said. 'Whatever happens, believe that the journey is worth taking, and then you will reach its end.' The bright singing came back into his voice, and he danced forward up the first dark slope, light on his elegant stick-like legs. 'Follow me now. There is only one way.'

Westerly called up after him, 'Have you been up here before?'

Peth's voice came back faintly, cheerfully. 'Have faith – have faith!'

He led them gradually up the beaten brown clay of the lower hills: a zig-zag way, across gaping fissures just narrow enough for a single step, along ridges that crumpled ominously as they put down their feet. There was no path, nor any sign of others having ever passed that way. Peth seemed simply to know which foothold would be safe, which slope would lead them up to another step, without dropping them into a ravine. Stepping lightly over cracks and boulders with his pad-footed jointed legs, he paused often to hold up his head. The antennae flickered, the eye-stalks swung to and fro, but he seemed too to be listening to some inner voice, a signal that Cally and Westerly could not hear.

As they climbed higher, the heat of the sun grew less oppressive; it no longer weighed on them like a huge heavy hand as it had in the desert valley. The mountains too began to change, the hard stone-studded clay giving way to glittering grey rock, steep and craggy. There were fewer stretches now where they could climb without using hands as well as feet.

Peth stopped on a ledge; in the sunlight his iridescent limbs shimmered like the body of a fish newly taken from the water. He folded his spindly legs beneath him. 'We will rest here.'

As she swung her pack down from her shoulder Cally found herself facing back the way they had come. She caught her breath.

The great valley lay spread below them, the mountain range at its further side only a dim blur on the horizon. There was no hint of green life on the plain now, only an immense grey sweep of land, blurring into white where the sand began. Very far away at one end of the valley, beyond the dunes, a brighter whiteness glimmered, merging into the haze where land met sky.

'The salt land,' Peth said, following her gaze.

Westerly said in awe, 'We've come all that way?' He looked out at the vast lifeless landscape. 'If it hadn't been for you –'

Peth sang a high note of laughter, though it seemed fainter and less bell-like than before. 'We are all one, Westerly-bound. The bird cannot fly without the air, the squirrel cannot climb without the tree. And the thinking creatures can neither fly nor climb except on each other's thoughts.'

Cally said curiously, 'When you were looking for us – how did you know we were there?'

'By thinking,' Peth said. 'The same thinking that made you sweetly gather those flowers.'

'Have some now.' Cally pulled Ryan's shawl out of her bag, laid it down on the ledge and carefully turned back the folds to reach the long bright blossoms she had picked for Peth. 'Oh no!' she said in distress.

The flowers were dead: brown and withered as dead leaves.

Peth's feathery antennae brushed her hand comfortingly. 'The gift was in the thinking.' he said. 'You must understand that always.'

Westerly was sitting chin on knees. staring out at the heat-shimmering sand in the valley below. He said. 'I've given up trying to understand anything.'

'Never do that,' Peth said.

'But – those shapes. With our faces. Chasing, and then gone. Real, and then nothing. Like the chessmen.'

Cally looked at him blankly. 'Our faces? Chessmen?'

'It was something that happened . . .' Westerly was looking intently at Peth. 'The ones following,' he said persistently. 'Who were they? Where did they go?'

Cally shivered. 'They're gone – I don't care who they were. Let's not think about them.'

But Westerly ignored her. He reached out a finger to one of Peth's antennae. 'You said not to give up trying to understand.'

The fragile antenna stroked his finger slowly, to and fro, absently, as if Peth were thinking. After a while the lilting voice said, 'Before you came to this world, you thought yourself pursued. Men chasing you.'

Westerly heard in his mind the hammering at the door, the shouts outside. 'Yes,' he said.

There was another pause. A breeze stirred the air where they sat. Peth said, 'This world that you are in now – it is not your own, but it is an image of your own. An echo. It may not look or sound the same as your world at any one time, not in the way that an image in a mirror looks the same. And the laws by which it exists may not be the same, sometimes, as those you know.'

Westerly thought of Lugan: *my task is to make sure that neither you nor anybody else break those laws . . .*

'But,' Peth said, 'it is an echo. It overlaps your world. *You* are the same in both worlds, just as you are the same person in your mind and your body. And so the things that happen in each world overlap.'

He stopped, and made an extraordinary sequence of soft clicking and whistling sounds. 'Oh dear,' he said plaintively, 'this is very difficult.'

Cally said, 'You make this country sound like a dream.'

'A waking dream,' Peth said. 'And between the two worlds, the familiar life and the waking dream, there are doors through which feelings may ride. Fear, fury, sorrow – delight and faith and despair. And on the backs of those feelings people may ride too. As the Lady Taranis is often in your world, riding many steeds, reaping a harvest that never ends. And as figures with the faces of your own guilts came from your world to this, riding on your fear.'

Westerly said, low and gruff, 'You mean if I hadn't been afraid of their coming, they wouldn't have come.'

'Look at it another way,' Peth said. 'If you had not had the courage to trust me, I could not have used the laws of this world to send them away. And your fear and needless guilt would be hounding you through all places and all times.'

He unfolded his long-jointed legs. 'We must go on. Up here, each nightfall will end our travelling. Look in your pack, Westerly. Now you will be climbing rock, and you should be roped together.'

Westerly said in surprise, 'How did you –?' He stopped, shook his head, grinned, and took the coil of rope out of his pack.

Cally looked at it nervously. 'D'you know how to do this?'

'Nope,' said Westerly cheerfully. 'But I know how to tie knots. Have to be bowlines round our waists, so they won't slip if someone falls.' He stood thinking for a moment, then uncoiled part of the rope and tied it round Cally's waist, about ten feet from the end. 'Wind the spare part round you and tuck it in,' he said. He found the other end of the line and tied it round his own waist in the same way.

Cally held up the coil of rope that now joined them. 'What do we do with this?'

'If I go first I ought to carry it, I suppose.'

She said mutinously, 'Why should you go first? You're so *macho*, West – big strong man lead, weak little woman follow. Like Hindu wives.'

'What about Hindu wives?'

'They're supposed to walk three paces behind their husbands, to show how inferior they are.'

'I don't think you're inferior, for heaven's sake,' Westerly said patiently. 'But I *am* stronger than you. I'd have much more chance of hanging on to you if you fell, than the other way round.'

'In that case you ought to be second on the rope,' Cally said. 'There's more strain there, if the first falls.'

Westerly sighed. 'All right. *All* right. You go first.'

'We still haven't decided what to do with the rope.'

Peth said impatiently, 'Carry the coil over your shoulder, so that it will fall loose easily, if need be.'

Westerly stared at him, a grin breaking. '*You*'ve used a rope?'

'I had time enough to work it out, while you bickered.' There was strain in Peth's voice, and for a moment they stood quiet, penitent. Then his laugh bubbled out again, and he moved off across the ledge and up a slanting rockface, picking his way as unconcerned as a fly on a wall.

Cally and Westerly had to struggle to keep up with him. Soon they were so intent on clinging to the mountain that they could do no more than glance up from time to time to make sure they were following his path. They would catch a quick sight of his head looking down at them; it was the brightness that they always saw, glinting out of the blue sky: the strange iridescent sheen like mother-of-pearl. And they heard his voice, singing in the wind.

'This way. Cally – over here. Put up your right hand.'

Cally reached, and found a secure jutting point of rock. Her fingers closed gratefully round it.

'Put your weight on your left foot, now, and reach up your left hand . . .'

With his help, Cally made her way snail-like up rock-faces that seemed smooth and impassable when she first looked at them. But she soon regretted her insistence on being the leader; Westerly, behind her, had only to mark and follow the holds that she – directed by Peth – had to grope for and agonizingly find. She strained and reached, testing each hold nervously, learning by trial and error not to hug the rock, not to cross her feet, not to hang from her arms but to push up her weight with her legs.

She said despondently to Westerly, as they stopped to rest, 'We're doing this all wrong.'

'Oh I don't know. I think we're doing pretty well.'

'Rubber soles are so slippery – we should have boots on. Any real climber watching us would have fits.'

'Look,' said Westerly practically, 'it's hard, but it's not Everest. For a real climber it probably wouldn't even be a real climb.'

Cally said, persisting, 'And this business with the rope isn't right either. It won't do anything except bring both of us crashing down, if one falls.'

133

'I've got an idea about that,' Westerly said tentatively. 'But –' He stopped.

'But you'd have to go first on the rope.'

Westerly said nothing.

Pride and reason jostled one another in Cally's mind. She sighed. 'All right.'

Peth called faintly from above, 'Are you ready?'

Westerly waved at him. He grinned at Cally. 'When we're on the ground again I'll walk three paces behind you,' he said.

She made a face at him. 'Go climb a mountain.'

'Hold tight.' He reached across and untied the rope from ner waist. 'Now you wait till I've climbed as far as I can get,' he said briskly, 'and then I make the rope fast and throw it down, and you tie it on and come up. Okay?'

Without waiting for an answer he swung himself up towards Peth. It was only when she was halfway up the rope to meet him that she realized he had neatly taken all the danger out of her own ascent, and put it into his own.

Peth flickered continually above them, calling directions, showing them foot-holds. His voice seemed fainter, as if he were tired, but he would not pause except when he felt Cally or Westerly needed a rest, or a drink of water. And then, when they had been climbing most of the day and the sun was high in the clear sky, they came to a place of such difficulty that Cally felt her forehead damp with fear as she looked at it.

Peth had scaled it easily in his sticky-footed insect stride, but there was no such way for human feet; he looked back at them anxiously, his antennae waving in a whirl of frustration. It was a chimney: the only way up from a broad sweeping ridge that had given them a deceptively easy climb for half an hour. Now two vertical rock-faces stretched up above their heads, with a three-foot gap between; up and up so high that they had to peer to see Peth in the bright

134

coin of sky at the top. Even the beginning of the chimney was high – higher than Cally's head. She looked up at it in horror. 'We can't possibly get up there!'

Westerly was pale. He called: 'Peth!'

But the thin high voice interrupted him, echoing down through the gap. 'Nothing is harder than this one – you will have no other like it. But it is the only way.'

Way . . . way . . . way, sang the echo in the chimney.

Westerly swallowed. He took off his pack, and stuck his head and arm through the coil of rope so that it lay diagonally across his chest. He looked at Cally with a strained grin. 'Got a strong back?'

She said unhappily, 'I think so.'

'So have I. We'll need mine to get me up through there, and yours to get me started. And then to get *you* through.' He looked at her doubtfully. 'I'm going to have to stand on you. Are you sure you're strong enough?'

'No,' Cally said. 'I shall break.' She planted her feet firmly apart and her hands on the rock wall, standing head down and back bent so that her body was like a step for Westerly to climb on. 'Will that do?'

'Bring your shoulders up a bit, and bend your knees.' Westerly was feeling at the wall for handholds. He wedged his fingers hard into the rock. 'Here we go!'

In a quick gasping swing he put one foot on Cally's knee, heaved on his hands and brought the other foot up to her shoulders, and his weight with it. Cally staggered, but held firm. He had both feet on her shoulders now, and both hands clinging to the rocky wall. His head and shoulders were in the chimney. He looked down. 'You all right?'

'Uh-huh.' Cally felt as if all her strength were screwed up into her back; there was none left for a voice.

'See if you can straighten up a bit. Just for a moment –'

Her muscles were screaming at her that they could not take one more ounce or instant of strain; but she pressed both hands against the wall, took a deep breath and straightened her back, raising her shoulders and Westerly with them. And in the next moment the weight was gone and she was lurching backwards, looking up to see Westerly wedged in the chimney, his back and hands flat against one rocky wall, his feet against the other, level with his hips.

He grinned down at her. 'Terrific! You didn't break!'

'But how –?' Her voice quavered; he seemed so perilously balanced that it made her feel sick to look at him.

'Physics,' Westerly said solemnly. 'Pressure. If I push hard enough sideways, I can go up instead of having gravity pull me down. Watch.'

Leaving one foot pressed forward against the opposite wall, he brought the other up under his bottom, raised his hands high on the wall behind him, and pressed with both feet and hands so that his body moved out into the chimney and up. Now the tucked-under leg was straight, and he was that much higher up the chimney. As if he were walking up the rock, he made the same upward swing again. And again, and again. Sometimes he rested, both legs locked straight against the far wall.

Cally's neck ached with looking. She sat down, curled tight in a ball, waiting desperately for the shout that would tell her Westerly had arrived at the top. When she could stand it no longer, she looked up just in time to see him hauling himself triumphantly over the edge. Then the circle of sky was blank.

She felt suddenly, horribly alone.

The rope came tumbling down the chimney, and Westerly's voice echoed after it. 'Cally! Send up the bags first – then tie the rope round your waist and tell me when you're ready.'

She tied the packs to the line, deliberately using a bowline knot for Westerly's benefit. Knots had been another of her father's favourite lessons. But when the line was back again and tied to her own waist. the security of the knot seemed small comfort. The vertical chimney of rock stretched endlessly above her head. Even if she could copy Westerly's climbing once she was inside it. how could he possibly pull her up through the first empty eight feet of space between ground and chimney? It was impossible: she would never get up there.

'Ready?' Westerly called.

Cally shouted in panic, 'No!'

His head was small and dark in the bright circle. 'What's wrong?'

She stood rigid, cold, paralysed. *I can't do it.* Then into her memory came a sudden image of Westerly taking the rope from her and climbing first, unprotected; and blurring into it. the look of the guardian fury on his face that had been the last thing she saw on the top of the tower. before Stonecutter's reaching hand sent her into the dark. Westerly's face and Lugan's merged in her mind. and Peth's voice with them. *Lugan's folk . . . we are Lugan's folk . . .*

She shouted back. ashamed and resolute. 'Ready!'

The rope drew her upward with an astonishingly strong, steady force. She was suspended in air, rising, and then she was between the rocky walls, pushing at them with her feet and hands and back, and yet drawn up all the time not by her own effort but by the rope. And the light grew brighter. and all at once her head and shoulders were out of the chimney. The rope slackened: she heaved herself out to sit on the edge of the rock, smiling. And Westerly was there laughing at her, coiling the rope into his hand. starting to tell her something, like a child with a secret. The sky was all around them, as if they were at the top of the world.

Then in a dreadful instant his face changed and he lunged backwards. his feet slipping from under him. and he fell. and there was nothing before Cally's face but the blue of the sky.

Chapter XV

A brightness flashed past her before she could move; it was Peth. He stood over her, leaning over the rim of the shelf of rock. eye-stalks bent down; through his spindly confusion of legs she saw the flat line of the rope, quivering. Tied to a rocky pinnacle beside her, it led to the edge over which Westerly had fallen. She crawled forward, and saw his body hanging a few feet below, limp, slowly turning.

'West!' It was a desperate shout; she knew there would be no response. But to her joyful amazement he turned his head and gave her a crooked grin.

'Stupid,' he said, croaking. 'Slipped.'

She reached for the taut rope. 'I'll pull you up.'

'No! Too hard. Catch – this.' Clutching the rope with one hand to steady himself, he groped down for the free end of line which dangled loose from his waist. Awkwardly, he flipped it up towards Cally. Twice she missed it; the edge of the shelf was slippery, and she dared not come too close. She lay flat, reaching out, and at the third attempt she caught the rope.

'Pull on that. I'll come up the other.' Westerly's voice was strained; the rope was cutting into his waist like wire, and he was giddy from the spinning sight of the huge drop below.

Cally pulled feverishly at the line, and felt him begin to rise towards the shelf. But her feet were slipping on the smooth rock; every pull took her closer to the edge. Frantically she looked round for a foothold, but could find nothing. She dropped on to her knees. 'Hang on, West!'

Peth's soft singing said, 'I will hold you.' He planted two of his long matchstick legs before her shoulders, and two next to her knees; she could hear the hiss of suction as the padded feet went down.

'Peth,' she said in confusion. 'You can't. You're too . . . I shall hurt you.'

'Too fragile?' The voice was weary but amused. 'Things are not what they seem, Cally. Pull the rope now, steady and hard.' He called, 'Come up, Westerly!'

Cally swallowed nervously. She heaved at the line, and began to slip forward to the edge of the shelf – but felt herself held firm by what seemed like rods of iron upright against her shoulders and knees. In wonder she pulled at the line, hand over hand, and Westerly came crawling over the lip of the rock and lay there, panting.

He saw Cally locked into position by Peth's thin shimmering legs, none of them thicker than her wrist, and he smiled weakly. 'Yes. That was how – we got you up the chimney so fast.'

Peth stepped delicately backwards, still looking as fragile as a large mosquito. He shone like gold now in the late sunlight. 'Westerly – are you well?'

'Thank you,' Westerly said. Cally saw that he was shaking all over. 'Thank you both. Thank you a lot.'

Peth said, 'A little further on . . . there is a place where we will spend the night . . . just a little further.' His voice sang faint and broken, as if he were gasping.

'You *have* hurt yourself,' Cally said anxiously. 'All that strain . . .' She looked from one to the other of them and was overwhelmed by an urge to protect. 'I don't think we should go anywhere, we should stop right here.'

'No time,' Peth said thinly. 'No time . . . We must go on – if Westerly –' He hovered restlessly.

'I'm all right now.' Westerly was on his feet, coiling the rope. 'Let's get there soon, then, so you can rest.'

But even when they had reached the sheltered corner of the mountain where they set up the tent for the night, Peth seemed still to be growing weaker. His voice had become softer, he moved more slowly, and in the moonlight he seemed somehow smaller and more insubstantial, in spite of the strength they now knew to be inside the fragile limbs.

'What is it, Peth?' Cally said gently. They sat outside the tent in its moon-shadow, with the whole valley spread silver-white beneath them. The air was cool. She and Westerly were nibbling slices of Ryan's food. 'There's something wrong, I know there is. Was it really not the pulling?'

'Oh no,' Peth said. He turned his head, and one feathery antenna brushed her cheek affectionately. 'I am like you or any other creature – best in my own place. And I am a thing of the desert. The high ground is not friendly to me.' He drooped, his voice fading like an echo.

'Wouldn't water help?' Westerly had the flask in his hand.

Peth folded himself up like a heap of collapsed sticks. 'No.' His voice was a singing whisper.

'You came up here to show us the way,' Cally said unhappily. 'You shouldn't have come. You should have stayed where you were meant to be.'

There was the flicker of a laugh. 'I decide where I am meant to be.'

Cally said, 'You should go back down tomorrow, first thing.'

'No,' Peth said. There was a flick of authority in his voice, even through the weakness. Cally sat silent.

Westerly was rummaging thoughtfully through his pack. He said, 'Peth, d'you know what this is?' He was holding out the small green glass bottle, unstoppered, on the palm of one hand.

Peth made a small whickering sound that was like an echo of the welcome they had heard him give the three

140

white bones, down in the desert. 'Lugan,' he said. He uncoiled his long slender proboscis and reached it out, and Westerly held the bottle steady while he drank. They saw the faint luminous glow begin to shine in his limbs again.

Cally said happily, 'We thought it must be medicine.'

'Of a kind,' Peth said. His voice was stronger. 'It will help. Good. Now we must rest.'

The night air was growing colder, and they made him sleep between them in the tent, for warmth. Peth hesitated, but he came in without protest and folded up into the strange resting position that made him seem like a pile of sticks.

When Cally woke in the morning, she found that she and Westerly each had one arm reached out, resting lightly round Peth. She looked at the folded insect-legs; in the early sunlight they had the familiar colour-swirling sheen that they had had before. Suddenly Peth rose, and smoothly unfolded all his six legs until he was standing over them. He sang into her mind, 'You will reach the top today, Calliope.'

'And you'll go back down to the desert – please?' Cally said anxiously.

But Peth only raised his voice, calling on a high ringing note, 'Wake up, Westerly-bound!'

He led them an odd twisting way up through the rocks. There were no perilous or even difficult places to climb now, but without his guiding they would instantly have been lost. The path he took was never straight, nor even always upward; it doubled back on itself, took wide improbable turns, sometimes led so far downhill that they seemed to lose as much height in five minutes as they had gained in fifteen. But Peth was sure and intent, never faltering, never pausing except to ask once in a while if they needed water or rest. He led them faster than ever before, urging them gaily on as if they were racing, playing a game; he seemed so lively, almost manic, that they began to feel their worrying about him had been foolish. It was only when they were within sight of the last peak of the mountain that they found how totally they were wrong.

They were walking diagonally across a broad slope, warmed by the high sun of middle-day, when Peth suddenly dropped to the ground. He did not trip; he simply collapsed into a heap, like a puppet loosed from its strings. When they ran to him he was whimpering softly, and his antennae were flickering feebly to and fro.

'Peth!' Cally said in terror. 'What is it?' She knelt down beside him and gathered the limp pile gently into her lap. The brightness was almost gone out of him: only a faint iridescence wavered in the thin, tough limbs.

Westerly pulled the green glass bottle from his pack, but it was empty.

'No – not this time.' Peth's voice was very faint. 'But it was enough. You have only one ridge to cross now. Go quickly. Up, and to the left. You will see.'

One antenna brushed Cally's hand, and then fell. His eye-stalks drooped. Cally could feel no movement in him. 'Peth!' She looked up in anguish at Westerly. 'Is he dying? What can we do?'

The voice sang so thin and distant that all at once they were very still, straining to hear. It seemed unrelated to Peth's body now, as if it were truly in the air. 'Calliope,' it said, whispering, 'Westerly – all things die, so that other things may live. We are Lugan's folk, we are a chain stretching through time. Each link must complete its circle, or there could be no chain. Do not mourn. Be glad that we are joined together – as all folk are, for always, whose lives have touched and held. Be glad of me.' The singing was fading, fading into the sky. 'Take my pride in you . . . to the sea . . .'

A small wind blew across the rocks, and very far off they heard one high sweet plaintive note like a calling, a trembling thread of sound; then it died away and there was nothing. All light was gone from the stick-like pile of limbs on Cally's lap. They were grey and lifeless, with no shape. as if they had never been Peth at all. She sat there crying unashamedly, the tears welling out of her eyes This one death contained within it all the others.

Westerly rubbed a hand over his own eyes. Then gently he moved the weightless heap from Cally's lap and knelt beside her. She bent her head.

'Cally,' Westerly said huskily. 'He told us to – to be glad.'

Cally sat hunched and miserable. 'If he hadn't come up here – if he'd stayed where he belonged –'

Westerly said, 'Listen. I thought that way about my mother at first. For a long time. If, if, if. You can't do it. you mustn't. it drives you crazy. You just have to say to yourself, somebody who loved me gave me a present – and the only way to say thank you is to use it.' He stood, and pulled her up after him. 'He told us to go. To go quickly. So we'll do that.'

'All right,' Cally said. She looked down. 'It seems so awful to just . . . leave him there.'

Westerly looked down at the small grey heap. He said gently, 'That's not Peth. Not now.'

'No.'

They went on up the slope. There was a clear way for climbing, beside a long fault where once a slab of rock had risen and formed a ridge. The breeze was stronger, blowing Cally's hair across her face, catching at the rope that still linked her to Westerly. They climbed in silence, using hands as well as feet, and then the ridge met a sheer rock-face and they knew they were at the point where Peth had told them to turn to the left. But before they turned, to make their way between other crags rising out of sight, a shared unspoken instinct made them look back.

And the wind whined across the mountain in a sudden

143

twisting eddy, and down on the ledge where they had left Peth's body, they saw a plume of grey dust puff out into the air and whirl away, down from the bleak mountains into the shimmering haze of the valley below.

There were clouds in the sky, travelling fast on the wind, white rough-edged pillows growing as they moved, blowing from the east. Westerly scrambled up towards the sky, with Cally close behind. They were on the last slope. Grey crags rose behind them, cutting off all sight of the valley, and for the first time in all their travelling they found themselves on a clear, well-defined path. It led diagonally up towards the peak of the final ridge, and the ridge itself was strange, unlike any part of the mountain they had crossed before. It rose into the air like a huge flat slab set on its side, and it seemed to be made of a softer rock, weathered and ancient, born out of an earlier age than the rest.

The rising path was cut firm and wide, yet Cally felt precariously balanced as she walked it; a sheer drop yawned at her left side, between the ridge and the rocks behind, and she dared not look down. She stared resolutely upward instead, at Westerly's swinging stride, and at last saw him stop, outlined against the blue sky and the rushing white clouds. She came up to stand beside him on the flat top of the ridge, and the wind sang in their ears.

They were looking out across a different world: a green land of rolling hills and wooded valleys, all its soft slopes dappled with cloud-shadows. Range after range of hills stretched out before them, purple and green and brown, merging into the misty horizon, but none was as high as the ridge on which they stood. And far out in the distance, between two of the rounded hilltops, they could see sparkling like a lost jewel the blue-white glint of the sea.

Westerly said softly, 'There it is.'

'It's a long way away.'

'But there it is!' He gave a sudden whoop, and grabbed her round the waist and hugged her. Laughing, Cally hugged him back, but then staggered.

'Careful! We're so high up –'

'Come on, then,' Westerly said promptly, gazing eagerly ahead. 'Let's find the way down.'

He drew her further ahead, to a curve in the path from which they could look down at the side of the mountain that belonged to the green world, and Cally looked, and gasped.

The huge sideways slab on which they stood was not merely the top of the hard hills they had climbed; on this side, it was the whole mountain. For hundreds and thousands of feet it dropped away, almost sheer, to the trees and slopes below. But its steepness was not forbidding; they could see the path winding down it in an endless wide series of hairpin bends, edged all the way with wildflowers and clumps of grass. On the slope between the zig-zags of the path, trees and bushes grew, rising out of land so steep that all their branches on one side brushed against the slanting earth.

Westerly said, grinning, 'Can you manage that?'

'I can manage anything that gets us down from here!' She ran ahead to find the first downward turn to the path, but the rope at her waist brought her up short. 'Oh. Sorry.' She untied the knot and coiled her part of the rope; Westerly took it from her.

'Shan't need that now,' he said cheerfully. He put it in his pack. The sunlight glimmered on the green glass bottle inside.

Westerly took the bottle out and held it up. He said, suddenly sober, 'Should we leave this here?'

Cally was silent for a moment. 'I think we should take it. It's like – part of him.'

'All right.'

They walked on together, round the first bend, where the path curved round to face the green seaward land.

Facing them, in the centre of the path, was a granite pillar. Cally stopped dead as she recognized it, clutching at Westerly's arm. Its top was carved into the familiar double face of the Lady Taranis, with the long hair rippling down, blending both sides. Then Cally breathed more easily: it was the gentle face which looked at them, smiling out in benison over the new land, towards the sea.

Westerly said softly, 'That's beautiful!'

'You know who it is?'

'Of course. She does look like that sometimes.' He moved forward. 'Come on. It can't do us any harm.'

Cally went on with him. But the air grew suddenly colder as a cloud came over the sun, and they heard a rasping, grinding sound, and felt the earth vibrate under their feet. In horror, they stared ahead. The pillar was turning. With a rumble of rock against rock it slowly moved round, gradually, relentlessly, and staring full at them with cold malignant eyes was the other face of Taranis.

They stared into the eyes, paralysed, unable to move a step further on the path. And out of a sky massed now with gathering grey cloud, snow began to fall, fast, white, blinding.

Chapter XVI

The sudden whirl of fat white snowflakes was so fast, so thick, that in an instant both Cally and Westerly were isolated in whiteness; they could see nothing, not even one another.

'Cally!' His voice was muffled; she could not tell where it came from. She groped at the place where he had been, and could not find him.

'West! Where are you?'

'Stand still – don't move. Don't move an inch. Just keep talking, and I'll find you. Talk – recite something – just so I can hear.'

Cally's mind was blank. The only thing that came into it was the last poem she had had to learn at school.

'And so the shortest day came, and the year died.
And everywhere down the centuries of the snow-white
     world

Came people singing, dancing,
To drive the dark away.
They lighted candles in the winter trees,
They hung their homes with evergreen,
They burned beseeching fires all night long –'

'I'll bet they did,' Westerly said. His arm was firm around her shoulders; she gasped in relief, clutching at him. The snow already lay thick on his jacket and his hair. It whirled into Cally's eyes; she knew that if he moved more than an arm's length away, she would lose sight of him again.

147

'The rope' she said.

'You're right.' He pulled it from his pack. and they roped themselves together once more. Westerly shouldered the coil and raised a hand. peering past her. 'Now – I found you from this way so the inside of the path is over there. Go slowly'

Hands out groping through the whirling snow. they moved forward until they found the rock. The cold bit through their clothes: Cally thought with longing of the warm jacket in her pack. Westerly tugged at the line round her waist. 'This way.'

He was moving cautiously downhill She held back. hissing at him. 'West, no! That face –'

Westerly said. low and determined. 'Lugan said to her you can't keep them if they wish to leave. Remember? Whatever awful things she dreams up. she can't *attack* us. Come on – just stay close to the rock.'

Blindly they shuffled down the slope. pressing against the rocky wall. shaking off the snow as it spread itself on them. Cally looked fearfully sideways for a glimpse of the stone pillar. but there was nothing. At last Westerly paused.

'There's a corner here – the first turn in the path. We can't go on like this – we'll go over the edge. Let's get the tent out.'

Fighting the heavy snow that came blanketing down into every fold and crevice. they had the thin, tough covering stretched over the frame just as the wind hit them. In a moment the snow was whipping at them as if driven by a blizzard: as if it were alive and had realized, just too late, that they should be stopped. The light tent-frame lifted and tipped; Westerly clutched at it. 'Quick! Get inside!'

They dived into the tiny space, trying to shake off the snow as they went. The wind howled over the tent as if in

148

frustration, and in moments the heavy snow was piling in drifts outside, covering the curving roof.

Cally was scooping out blown snow before it could melt. 'The wind helped us once – now it's the opposite.'

'The same with everything. The sun, the river.'

'They belong to her.'

'But to Lugan too,' Westerly said. He pulled out his blanket, and Ryan's jacket and shawl for Cally, and they wrapped themselves like cocoons.

'Lugan's folk,' Cally said. 'We keep hearing that we're Lugan's folk. But Lugan's dead.'

'I don't think so. I don't think she can kill him. That wave – it was as if they were playing some terrible game.' He stopped abruptly, hearing his own words, remembering the game of chess.

The wind hurled an icy spatter of snow against the roof of the tent. They sat hunched in the dim, cold light that filtered through from the whirling grey-white world outside. There was a layer of darkness at the base of the tent, where the snowdrifts were rising.

Cally felt suddenly dreadfully tired, as if the life were draining out of her. She said miserably, 'We'll never get away. Every time we start to get somewhere, she stops us.'

'We know where the sea is,' Westerly said. 'We saw it.'

'That was just to make it worse. To show us what we couldn't have. And then she sent the snow, and it's getting worse and worse and we're never going to get out . . .' Her voice tailed away.

Westerly said firmly, 'We're just going to wait it out. It can't go on for ever. You'd feel better if you weren't so tired – lie down, come on. Get some rest.' He folded the flap of his pack over its knobbly contents and pushed it under Cally's head for a pillow as she lay curled up on the tent floor. 'Are you warm enough?'

'I'm all right.' Cally's voice was muffled, her back turned

149

towards him. 'Oh West. You should have gone on your own, that time you wanted to.'

'You crazy? Who'd have pulled me up when I fell over the rock?'

'You wouldn't have fallen over, if you'd been on your own.'

'I wouldn't have trusted Peth either. So now where would I be?'

Cally made a small snuffling sound that might have been crying; he reached out a hand to her back, then hesitated and withdrew it again.

She said, 'You've done much more for me than I have for you. And there's all the others who've done things, just to get us to the sea, and what's happened to them? That dragon was killed – and Lugan – and Peth –'

Westerly said positively, 'Lugan's not dead.'

'We don't know that.' Cally's voice was thick with misery. 'There's no point in it all. My mother and father are dead and there's no point in anything.'

Her shoulders were shaking. In swift overwhelming concern Westerly slid down and put an arm round her from behind, holding her close to him. 'Don't, love. Come on, Cal.'

Choking, she shook her head violently. 'There's no point, there's no point. I just want to go to sleep and not wake up any more.'

Westerly felt desperate to comfort her, and at the same time his body stirred at the closeness of her, at the curve of her breast against his hand, and the smell of her hair. He made himself bring his arm back from holding her, and he stroked her hair and kissed the back of her neck. 'We're going to the sea, Cal, we're going to get there. Remember what Peth said? Whatever happens, he said, believe that the journey is worth taking, and then you will reach its end.'

Snow thudded heavy against the roof of the tent, falling in a wave from the rock above, and the curve of the roof swelled down ominously towards them. Cally did not move. She said in a small voice, 'It's never going to stop.'

He cupped his hand over her shoulder, his face against her hair. 'Oh Cally, Cally –' Lying close, he rocked her gently as if she were a small child; but he was fiercely aware that she was not a child, and he would have turned her round to his own wanting body if his own words had not still been echoing in his head. *Remember what Peth said . . . remember what Peth said . . .*

What had Peth said? He knew the small insistent voice must have some purpose, but he could not understand. What had Peth said that could help stop the snow?

Now listen well, and always remember. There is a calling you may do . . .

'Cally!' Westerly shouted.

He swung upright, and scrambled to his feet, lurching against the tent wall. It swung, heavy with snow. Cally sat up, her eyes wide and frightened. The look on her face caught at him, but he was too excited to stop.

'I've got it, I've got it!'

He bent beside her to his pack, and scrabbled inside. Pulling out the three white bones, he knelt down and ripped open the fastening of the tent-flap. Snow came whipping in on the wind, and Cally made a small sound of distress – but then stopped herself, watching, hunched under her shawl.

Carefully Westerly planted the three bones in the heavy snow outside, standing them upright in a triangle, pointing at the sky. Then he clambered out of the tent, stepping over them. The wind blew his hair into his eyes; in a moment snow was clinging to his shoulders, driving cold down his neck. He stood there happy and oblivious in the whirling white world, and he said, loudly and clearly, like a calling:

> *'Water and fire and air, by these we live,*
> *By rain and sun and wind.*
> *Oh sky, I am in need.*
> *Send me the sun.'*

The wind dropped. With the end of its howling, echoing shriek, silence fell on the snow like a blanket. Holding her breath, Cally crawled forward to the door of the tent, and saw Westerly standing rigid, legs apart, arms spread, gazing up at the sky as the snowflakes fell into his eyes.

But the snowflakes were growing less, and somewhere in the whiteness a brighter glow was beginning, somewhere out beyond the path where the tent stood. Then out there, as they watched, there was a blaze of sunlight and a flash of blue, and they looked up, and saw the huge bank of grey cloud that had covered their world boiling like steam, curling in on itself, rushing away across the sky as if driven by a great wind. Yet they felt no wind. They felt only the warmth of the sun, embracing them, hanging fiery in a clear sky, glittering on the still snow that lay all around them on rock and path and tree.

Westerly looked at Cally, and spread his hands.

'Peth,' he said. 'He showed me how.'

'It's gone,' Cally said in wonder. 'It's all gone.' She stood up, slowly 'Oh West. I'm sorry. I was . . . in a pit.'

'Hey,' he said. 'Taranis put you there.' He swung round to the tent. 'Come on, let's get this off.' He began cheerfully sweeping armfuls of snow down to the ground.

Cally helped him. When the roof was clear they paused, looking over the mounded edge of the path. Between the green hills on the horizon there was the glimmer of the sea still, and below it the distant land was hazed with green and purple and brown as it had been before. But over all the mountain the snow lay thick and glittering, mounded white on every branch of every tree, masking the crevices of the steep dropping hillside with smooth rounded drifts.

'It's so beautiful,' Cally said. 'And a few moments ago it could have killed us.'

'Speciality of the country,' Westerly said. 'The murderous beauty, the beautiful murderer. Just like the owner of the property.' He looked down the precipitous hillside, all its angles smoothed now by snow. 'And we can't even get away yet. The path's buried.'

But by the time they had dismantled the tent, discovered that they were hungry and eaten the last of Ryan's food, the path was clear. Looking down, they could see it written in a dark zig-zag pattern through the white snow, as if the beaten earth had itself grown warm enough to melt its way through to the sun. Rivulets of water ran down the path from the dripping, dwindling snowdrifts.

Bare-armed in the hot sun, they set off down the hillside to the green land waiting below.

Chapter XVII

Halfway down the hill, they heard the sound of water moving much faster than the tiny trickle about their feet; a spring ran out of the rock, cascading down in a long miniature waterfall. Twice their criss-crossing path led across its course, so that they ran laughing through the spray. At the foot of the hill the fall splashed into a deep green pool, irresistible in the hot sun. Cally and Westerly swam, yelping at the coldness of the water; washed the dirtiest of their clothes with the soap from Westerly's pack, and spread them on the bushes to dry.

Cally sat listening to a bird calling unseen from the trees overhead: *chink-chink, chink-chink*, clear and bright, as if it were trying to rival the splash of the waterfall. She said, 'It's ages since we heard birds sing.'

Westerly was lying on his back in the sun with his eyes closed. He opened them a slit. 'Want to know something weird?'

'Everything's weird.'

'Well. Yes. But I swear the sun's hardly moved since we were on top of that ridge.'

Cally looked up; then all around, at the long lush grass and full-leaved trees. Tall red spikes of flowers grew at the water's edge, and from a tangle of bushes nearby the heavy scent of honeysuckle drifted through the air.

'It's summer. A long summer day that just goes on and on.'

Westerly closed his eyes again. 'I'd like to lie here for ever.'

Cally said slowly. 'I suppose we could, too. That's just what she wanted.'

He sat up, frowning. 'You think we're still in her country?'

'Where else could we be?'

'I don't know. I just felt we'd . . . left it behind. Up there.'

'I think it reaches all the way to the sea,' Cally said. 'This is the same as the other part, really. It's like her two faces.'

Westerly looked at her. She sat hugging her knees, wearing the fine-woven white blouse and brown woollen skirt that had been in Ryan's pack. Her newly-washed hair was loose over her shoulders, glinting in the sun. He wanted to touch it.

Cally sensed his gaze; she felt a prickling down her spine, as she had earlier when she had watched him lying face down on the grass, brown-skinned, wearing nothing but a frayed pair of jeans. She scrambled up and went to feel the clothes spread on the bushes. 'They're dry.'

Westerly got reluctantly to his feet and stuffed his clothes into his pack as she handed them over. He said, 'At least we can follow water to the sea again.'

From the green pool a stream ran quietly away through grasses and small trees, and the path that had led them down the mountain curved round and went on unbroken at the stream's side. They walked together through the sunshine, leaving the music of the waterfall behind, hearing only the lazy hum of insects and the bright chirruping of birds who seemed to follow as they went, darting overhead from tree to tree.

Westerly said abruptly, 'You don't really *know* your parents are dead.'

They walked on in silence for a while. Then Cally said quietly, 'Yes I do. I do now. It's not so terrible as you seeing your mother die, but it's the same.'

'But Taranis coming for them doesn't mean they . . .

Taranis isn't real. Nothing from this world is real.'

'You came into it through a real door,' Cally said. 'I came into it through a real mirror.'

'Hum,' Westerly said. He pulled at a stem of grass as he walked, and chewed on it.

Cally said, 'That's what you always say when you know something's right even though you wish it wasn't.'

'What?'

'"Hum."'

Westerly smiled, but he said soberly, 'I do wish it wasn't right.' He fell a few paces behind her as they passed a low-hanging tree, its branches stroking the stream. 'Cally – if you know you won't find them, why are you still going to the sea?'

'Because Ryan gave me a message to take, and I promised,' Cally said. Then she added, very low, so that behind her back he could only just hear, 'And because you're going.'

He caught up with her again and took her hand, and they went on along the path, beside the murmuring water, walking with their own thoughts, until ahead of them the sound of the water seemed to change, and grow. The sky was clear blue overhead, the sun still high; rounded green hills rose in the distance on either side of them as if they were travelling through a broad valley. Then they came out of the trees that fringed the path and saw that before them their small stream poured itself into a wide slow-moving brown river, and that the path too merged into a wide stone-paved road. Road and river stretched ahead, winding gently, masked by trees so that they could not see what lay on the horizon. But they could see that the road was filled with people, walking.

Cally and Westerly paused, wondering. There was no sound but the song of the birds and the slow-speaking river; not one of the figures walking down the road spoke to any other, and their feet seemed to make no noise. But the broad highway was crammed with them, hundreds of them, thousands, walking, a long crowd flowing as if it too were a river. There were children, old men and women, people of every age and size and race. At the nearest edge, passing them, they saw in succession an old man wrinkled as a prune, wearing a turban and white robes, a woman with fair skin and yellow hair, a long-haired boy their own age in a nail-studded leather jacket, a tall black man in a business suit, a small Japanese girl jumping rope – all walking, together and yet separate, gazing ahead.

Westerly said tentatively to the man in the suit, 'Sir –' But he walked by as if he had not heard; no one in all the endless moving throng gave a glance to the two of them, standing there amazed and watching. They walked by, silent and slow, and on all the faces there was the same expression: a dazed look of wondering discovery, happy and bemused.

The river murmured, the birds sang, and high overhead a small hawk hung in the air, motionless, hovering.

Westerly and Cally stood astonished, watching the broad river slowly flowing, the river of people moving silently along at its side. They could not see where the highway came from, or where it ended; it reached on into the distance and all its length was filled with the endless polyglot crowd. The same instinct took both of them at the same moment, and they stepped forward on to the surface of the road and joined the walkers, keeping pace with them, hand in hand.

They never knew the time of the walking. Once they had joined the crowd, it seemed to them as if the road were itself moving forward, flowing as the river flowed, and they were caught up in a kind of quiet exhilaration, and saw on one another's faces the same look that was on all the faces all around. On through the green country they walked, among their silent companions, and gradually they began to feel a freshness in the lazy summer air, and to hear the sound of seagulls crying, distant in the sky.

They saw that the river beside which they walked was growing broader, filling the valley, edged now with flat banks of sand on which small long-legged seabirds stalked, dipping their straight-beaked heads down to the shallows as Peth had bent his head to the flowers. The sand lay golden in the sun, the river now was blue as the sky. The voices of the gulls were louder, a plaintive curving calling, and they could see the white wings flocking, wheeling, further ahead.

Then they rounded a bend in the river, and looking down its course they saw open before them the flat blue horizon of the sea.

The road climbed; the bobbing heads of the crowd were rising, ahead. Forced to the edge of the valley by the broadening river, the highway was carved here into a ledge of the hillside, and as the crowd flowed along it, Cally and Westerly could see the sea and the great blue-gold estuary of the river set out below them like a promise.

On the road itself, grey roofs were rising now at either side: small stone houses lined the wide street. There was no sign of any occupants, but bright flowers were massed everywhere round their doors, blue and gold and red and white, fuchsias and hydrangeas and black-eyed Susans, roses and wallflowers, sweet-scented, golden-brown.

The gulls cried strong and loud; they heard the creak of boats at their moorings, the clash of metal, and voices calling; and ahead of them was the harbour.

It was huge. Hundreds of boats lay at anchor, or tied up at the long jetties. There were long and sleek streamlined cruise-boats, there were tall-masted square-riggers; there were junks, dhows, dinghies, like a chart of all boats from all ages and all seas. But between the boats and the thronging crowd, an immense stone gateway stood.

158

The white stone gleamed dazzling in the sunlight, so that it was hard to tell how far the gateway reached; they could see only that it was divided by many entrances, and that each member of the moving crowd ended his or her long walking at one of these. They could not see what happened beyond. They drew nearer, the white stone walls reaching high over their heads. At each entrance a man or woman stood, with one hand on a round white stone set in the wall. Cally looked puzzled at one face after another, all these greeting guardians. She saw a man with a dark pointed beard, another with shoulder-length hair and a gold circlet round his forehead; a woman with green eyes and a smile like sunlight, a twinkling man with a square white beard and grizzled hair: they all looked oddly familiar, and yet she could not remember having seen any of them before.

Every man or woman or child who approached one of the gateways spoke his or her name, and then the name of a country. The round stone flashed golden for a moment, and the guardian at the gate smiled in welcome and reached out both hands. And the arrival, dazed still but smiling, took the hands for a moment and then went in; through the gate of the harbour, towards the ships.

'Guy Leclerc, France.'

'Ramon Chavez, Guatemala.'

'John Ndala, Zimbabwe.'

'Danny Kelly, United States.'

'Wu Yi-ming, China.'

'Sarah Farr, England . . .'

The gulls wheeled overhead, a salt breeze blew in from the sea. Cally and Westerly moved forward to the nearest entrance, and a tall dark-eyed woman there smiled at them, beckoning. They went to her, and stood under the white stone arch. Cally began, 'Calliope –'

The round stone flashed red, and suddenly over all the arching gateways and through the air of the harbour there was a furious jangling of alarm bells Lights blazed. sirens wailed. and crashing down on all four sides of Cally and Westerly came four gleaming white walls. They slammed into place and stood solid and firm. enclosing them in a tight white square. a cell of stone.

Chapter XVIII

The silence was sudden and total. Cally and Westerly could see nothing but the white walls. It was as if they had been wrenched out of life.

But as they stared at the enclosing room there was a blurring, a mistiness all around, and the walls seemed to retreat until the space in which they stood was far larger, far higher: a great hall walled with white mist. And the mist at one end of the hall glowed golden, and they saw a tall figure, cloaked in gold. walk out of it towards them.

Westerly leapt forward. 'Lugan!'

Cally followed, in hope and relief edged with an odd feeling of shyness – but then she stopped. Out of the mist behind Lugan, gleaming cold as moonlight, came the Lady Taranis. Her light hair streamed loose over her blue robes.

Lugan was smiling at them. 'Well done,' he said. 'For enduring your journey, and now this last . . . astonishment. You are my folk indeed.'

Westerly said triumphantly. 'I knew you weren't dead.'

'Why couldn't we go through the gateway?' Cally said. She was dazed, half her mind still held by the image of the silent walking crowd, and the ships waiting on the sea.

'Because you are in life, Calliope,' Taranis said. There was a warmth in her face and voice that caught at them in spite of their mistrust. 'Because you and Westerly belong still to your own world, if you wish it. But those other travellers have left it behind.'

Lugan said, 'The gateway is for them – not for you, not yet. And so the alarms rang when you tried to pass.' He looked at their uncomprehending faces. 'Come,' he said abruptly. 'We will show you the country, so that you may understand.'

As Cally and Westerly drew level with him he swung round, holding his cloak by its edge, flinging out both arms so that he seemed to enfold them and Taranis in two great golden wings. He drew them forward into the white mist that swirled where there had been a wall, and through the mist into brightness. And they were standing out under the blue sky on a grassy headland high above the sea, with the sweep of that limitless flat horizon before them, and at their backs the rolling green hills and plains inland. Below on the edge of the sea was the bustling harbour; faintly they could hear the cries of the gulls, and see the glimmer of the broad white gate where the thronging travellers passed through to reach the ships. One tall-masted schooner was putting out to sea as they watched; they could see its sails take shape and fill as it drew away from the land.

Inland, they saw the shining course of the river, and beside it the broad highway filled with moving figures. But they could not see where the highway came from; it seemed simply to begin, somewhere in the misty hills, as if it burst from under the ground like a spring.

Taranis pointed down at the flowing crowds. 'Those are the travellers from your world,' she said. 'All those who were glad to be alive, but who in your terms are dead. They pass in their thousands every day, and the crowd never grows less. But not all choose the journey to the sea. Many are so weary, after a long life and a hard one, that when it is over they wish only to sleep. So sleep is what they are granted, and their spirits drift out in peace through the gentle darkness, and lie resting on the winds that blow between the bright stars, forever.'

Lugan said, turning his lean, handsome face to the hills, 'And those who live but would take no joy from living, or who sought to destroy life, are caught forever between life and death in the manner of the Stone People. Devoted still only to destruction, and to the building of Stonecutter's endless, meaningless walls.' A hard note came into his voice. 'To the service only of the Lady Taranis.'

She said softly, 'I have two faces, certainly. But so do you.'

He paid no attention; he looked down at the crowded harbour and the blue-green sea, and his voice grew warm again. 'All the rest, all those travelling down there, are those who loved their lives even through the hardness of them. Lugan's folk. Those who took pleasure in the world, and gave it – who sometimes gave even their lives, for the sake of others. On that joy they travel to the edge of the sea, and they may put out across it to my islands, the land of the Tir n'An Og, the ever-young – where my folk may live without hurt, without change. It is a different kind of living, a different delight, lapped by the sea of time. And – my sister may not come there.'

He glanced at Taranis, with a mixture of love and wariness in his tawny eyes. Wondering, Cally and Westerly looked at them both, and for the first time saw a hint of likeness between his strong, clear profile and the beautiful fine-boned face in its glimmering frame of silver hair. Taranis looked back at them.

'Do you not know us?' she said. 'Do you not know us yet, in this our country? I am Death, my children. I rule this world just as I rule your own, I have followed you everywhere here, just as I follow you there. But Life rules with me. He is my brother and my father and my son, and all of them are called Lugan. We are one, even in our opposition.'

They stared. Cally saw again in her mind the huge wave rushing up the river to the lock, heard the shrill cold triumph in Taranis' laughter as the brown water swirled round Lugan's head. She said, 'But you tried to kill him!'

163

Taranis' blue eyes glinted, and for a moment Cally felt deathly cold, as she saw a flash of the dreadful second face on the guardian pillars. But Lugan's deep calm voice broke in.

It is the nature of things, Cally. Death ends life, and life is renewed. My lady is bound to me, for without life how could there be death? But so too I am bound to her – as the leaves must die in winter so that the new buds may swell in the spring. In a world set within Time, there can be no beginning without an end.'

'So it goes in the Country of Life and Death,' Taranis said, and so the echo of it is played out in your world. And once in a very great while a Cally or a Westerly is brought by chance from one world to the other, to see the two of us plain.'

Westerly was sitting on the grass with his chin on his knees, watching the ships slowly moving out across the sea. By chance?' he said bitterly. 'Her mother died. So did mine.

'And you were driven by the force of your grief,' Taranis said, 'which is still with you, and which only time will take away. Yes. But it was by chance that each of you found the old power of crossing between worlds – you through your mother's knowledge, Cally through her selkie hands. That power comes from laws which we do not control, or even understand. We did not bring you here.'

Lugan cocked an eyebrow at her quizzically. 'But once they *were* here –'

'Yes, I would have kept them.' she said petulantly. 'Small wonder if I want company. I am Death, and I am lonely You care only for your folk.'

'There are two of them here that I care for,' he said. 'And since they have followed this long journey to the sea, they have the charge of their own lives now. They are out of my control or yours. They may choose where they will go.'

Very well.' Taranis said. Her blue eyes were remote. 'They will choose your way, of course. The land where I may not come. The land of eternal summer, where nothing passes, or ends, or begins. For them, I am nothing but cruelty and grief and pain, a losing, a sense of darkness. And indeed I am all those things, sometimes. But I wish the journey might have taught them' – her eyes sought Cally's, deliberate, gazing – 'that I am also your twin, that I have my other face. That it is the endings that make the beginnings. Sunrise, flowers in the desert, blossom on the apple trees.'

Cally looked back at her, wondering.

Westerly jumped to his feet. 'We can really go where we want to?'

'Yes,' Lugan said.

'I promised I'd find my father,' Westerly said. 'He's on an island.'

Taranis held Cally's gaze for a last moment, then turned to him. 'Your father is of Lugan's folk,' she said, 'and so he is in the islands to which the ships sail. And so is your mother, and so are Cally's parents. Is that where you wish to go?'

'Of course,' Westerly said firmly. He hitched his pack over his shoulder, and grinned at Cally. 'Right?'

Cally said nothing. She looked out at the sea, and saw, away beyond the headlands, waves breaking over a long black outcropping of rock. Unconsciously she rubbed the palms of her hands.

Taranis stood tall, straight and beautiful in the sunlight, and with one arm she swept out her blue cloak like an embracing wing, as Lugan had done. 'Come to the ships then,' she said, and her cloak swirled round Westerly, and they disappeared. The last flicker of an image that Cally saw was the dark eyes wide in his brown face, looking back at her.

She heard the seagulls calling faint and plaintive in the clear sky, out over the sea.

Lugan said, 'Well, Calliope?'

She looked up at him; at the laugh-lines sober and straight now in the lean face, and the sunlight gilding his hair. She thought: *he looks like the sun.*

'I made a promise too.' she said.

'I know.'

Lugan took her hand. He raised his other arm and pointed down at the black rocks that rose wet-gleaming out of the sand below. There was a rushing of wind, and a singing in Cally's ears, and she found herself down in a mist of sea-spray with the smell of salt in the air.

She stood on the rocks; at her feet the dark sea rose and fell in great rolling swells, like the huge heart-beat from which Snake had come to them, under the earth. She found herself breathing to the rhythm of it. The wind blew in her face, and faint within it she heard voices, a high wordless singing; and down in the swelling water she saw shining black shapes swimming, diving, curving over and under one another in a sinuous, joyous blur of movement. In that too she felt she found Snake. His words echoed out of the past: *your life's your own − follow your own way, and enjoy it:* she felt somehow that the meaning of them was down there with the dark creatures revelling in the waves. and she felt an itching ache in the palms of her hands, as strong as pain calling her down to join them.

Dark eyes looked at her from the sea, where a head broke through the waves as the biggest of the turning bodies rose and wheeled and splashed back again. The face was whiskered, and the teeth flashed white as if in a smile, but it was not the head of a man, or of Snake. It was a great grey seal, darkened by its sleek wetness; again and again it dived and rose and broke through the waves to look at her.

Cally gazed into the huge liquid black eyes as they rose again. She said softly, 'Don't despair. She will come.'

In a gleaming dark flash the seal swerved and dived and was gone, and behind her Cally heard a voice calling.

'Cally! Calliope!'

It was a shout, but faint and far away. Cally turned to face the long golden sweep of the beach, and the tiny shapes of the ships in the distance beyond, and she saw Ryan running down the beach towards the sea. She seemed no longer old and worn, but young, running like a girl: her hair blew out long and straight in the wind, and she was carrying a black bundle in her arms. She shouted indistinctly to Cally again, and waved.

Cally's hands were calling her toward the sea.

'Come with us!' Ryan called. 'Come home!'

Cally clenched her hands together, and felt the throbbing in the palms. She swung round and looked down again at the glistening, swirling seals playing in the waves; a face rose up laughing at her, and this time she knew that it was Snake.

The sea and the spray and the voices of the waves all called to her; the rhythm of the swells was the beating of her own heart. She turned back irresolute to look at Ryan, and saw her running into the sea, fully clothed, holding the black bundle to her. Further out in the waves she saw the big grey seal swimming, waiting, a dark flashing shape in the green water and the white spray.

Ryan called and waved to her once more, laughing, excited, and then she dived into the waves and disappeared. And when Cally looked again for the big dog-seal she saw not one but two dark sleek figures, curving and playing in the sea.

Without thinking of what she was doing, she turned her face up to the sky in longing, and she heard herself call out, 'Oh Westerly! Where are you?'

Lugan's voice said gently at her side, 'Yes. That's why you didn't go with her, isn't it? Why you held back from the wanting, and the inheritance.'

Cally looked up. He was standing beside her on the rocks,

his golden robe wrapped round him by the wind. He reached out and touched her clenched fists, and Cally realized that all the shouting pain had gone out of them. Slowly she opened her hands, holding them out before her, and saw that each palm was smooth and unscarred, as if the thick, horny skin of the selkie had never been there.

She stared at them, wondering.

'You chose not to use it,' Lugan said. 'So it is gone.'

Cally said uncertainly, 'Was that the wrong thing to do?'

'Of course not. There is no right or wrong, here. There are only different ways of living.'

Cally looked at the dark, heaving sea. She could see nothing there now but the waves. 'Are the selkies your folk too?'

'Oh yes,' he said. He laughed. 'They are like Snake – all joy in their element, and no doubts or fears. You carry that in your blood, if you will listen to it. Ryan feared no one but Stonecutter – and when Taranis took away his powers, Rhiannon of the Roane was free to take back her skin that he had hidden from her, and come home here to the seals.'

Further out on the sea, small and distant in the mouth of the harbour, another ship was moving towards the misty horizon where the islands lay. Cally said bleakly, 'Westerly must be on board that one.'

'Perhaps,' Lugan said.

He was looking down along the flat golden expanse of the beach, standing tense and somehow expectant, his lean face expressionless. Cally glanced too at the long stretch of sand, shimmering in the heat of the sun – and then she stood very still, staring.

A figure was running towards them, running in a straight line along the beach from the direction of the harbour. Dwarfed at first by distance, it grew gradually clearer, loping along at a steady unbroken pace. Cally gazed at the runner for a long silent time before she was certain. It was Westerly.

He ran steadily, without pausing, without looking up, until he came to the single line of Ryan's footprints on the sand. Then he stopped at once. He stood staring at them for a moment; then flung himself down to the point at which they disappeared into the sea. Watching his taut figure peering at the waves, Cally suddenly realized what he must be thinking.

She shouted, 'West! *West!*'

His head jerked up, and he turned. As he began to run again, Cally clambered down over the edge of the rocks towards him, slipping and slithering on seaweed and wet stone. She jumped down on to the sand just as Westerly came running up to her, to pause breathless and panting, a few feet away, looking at her.

His face and his shirt were damp with sweat. He said, haltingly, but with a smile breaking, 'I – couldn't go without you.'

Cally was laughing; she felt delight bubbling up in her like a spring. Instinctively she flung her arms round him, feeling the length of his body against her own, her face pressed against his neck. Westerly held her for a moment and then drew back. His hands were holding her shoulders. He said, grinning at her, 'Hello, Cal.'

Ceremonially he kissed her on both cheeks; then paused for a second, and kissed her on the mouth.

Neither of them was laughing then; they stood staring at one another, shaken by discovery.

Lugan said, behind them, 'Welcome back, Westerly.' He was smiling at them, the tawny eyes bright; he looked, Cally thought suddenly, like a father proud of his children.

Westerly let his hands drop from Cally's shoulders, but took her hand. He said to Lugan, 'Wherever we go, can we go together?'

'Oh indeed,' Lugan said. The smile faded as he looked at them, and the lines of his lean face grew oddly tense. 'But then you face the biggest of all the choices, my children.' He hesitated, turning his head to the sea as if he were looking for something. The sun was huge out there, sinking to the horizon; his hair and his robe glowed in its red-gold light. There was the flash of a swifter light for an instant, flicking past them, and they saw that from the harbour beyond the beach, the long white beam of a lighthouse was swinging steadily round over sea and land.

Lugan said, 'You may go over the sea, if you choose, with those other travellers. You may go to my islands, to join your parents and all the memories, and you may go together. But you will go as children, as you are now, and you will never change. Time does not pass, in that land. Because Death may not go there, nothing alters, nothing fades – the old do not die, the young do not grow old. And those who are on the edge of leaving childhood behind them, as you are, will never cross that edge, but live on it for ever.' He looked from one to the other of them. 'Which is to say, that if you love one another, as I think perhaps you do, the loving too will remain on the edge, suspended, never growing up.'

Westerly and Cally did not look at one another, but each was as fiercely conscious of the other's hand as if all the blood of both their bodies circulated through those two jointed palms.

'Oh, you will be happy enough,' Lugan said, 'because you will not know. Where there is no change, there is neither promise nor disappointment – only content. And the wisdom of not wanting more than it is possible to have.'

Westerly said slowly, 'I don't know that I want to be wise. Or contented. At any rate not yet.'

'Nor do I,' Cally said. 'Maybe not ever.'

Lugan said nothing. The sun had dropped below the horizon; the daylight was dying. The long beam of the lighthouse swept across the dark sea, flashed brightness at them for a second, and was gone again. In its light Cally saw that Lugan was smiling.

She said, 'If we don't go to the islands – what then?'

He turned his head to her; she could see the tawny eyes glinting even in the half-light.

'Then you will go back to the world from which you came,' he said, 'and it will be as if you have never left. You will each go back to grief and loss, but you will have the strength to survive them, for echoing at the back of your minds – not quite seen or heard, nor quite apprehended – will be all those things that you have learned on your journey here. Like the leaves on the trees each year, you will grow and change. And indeed, you may never find wisdom or contentment in that world into which you were born – but you may if you are lucky see a light that blazes far more brightly, even though it must in the end burn itself out.'

Westerly said persistently, 'But will we be –'

'Together?' Lugan said. 'No. Not at first. You go back to the different countries from which you came. You each have your own lives to attend to. Neither of you will be conscious of missing the other, because the memory of what has happened through this gap in time, in this country, will be buried deep in your minds.'

His cloak flapped in the breeze blowing out to sea. The lighthouse beam swept over them once more.

'But I promise you,' he said, 'that you *will* meet, in that world, before long. And that when you meet, you will remember – and begin again. To live together through all the discoveries and lovely astonishments that go with the grief and the pain, in a land ruled by Death.'

Cally said, 'That was what she meant, wasn't it? *It is the endings which make the beginnings. Sunrise, flowers in the desert, blossom on the apple trees.*'

'Yes,' Lugan said. 'As dust blows from a mountain ledge, so that two children may live.'

Westerly said suddenly, 'Peth would have wanted us to go back.'

'Peth *knew* we'd go back,' Cally said. 'Lugan –' She could see his face again; there was a curious brightening in the sky above the rocks. 'What happened to Peth?'

'He wished for sleep,' Lugan said. 'He was very tired. Peth was the oldest of my folk, as old as the desert itself – he had been in life for a long, long time. So he sleeps in his desert, under the stars.'

Brightness was all around them suddenly, as the moon rose gleaming over the dark rocks at their side. Cally saw Lugan's shadow lying long and black on the flat sand; then she clutched Westerly's hand more tightly.

He turned to her. 'What's the matter?'

'Look. You and I – we have no shadows.'

The sand at their feet was bright and empty. Lugan laughed softly. 'The moon belongs to the Lady Taranis,' he said, 'and knows that already, in your hearts, you are no longer here. Come then, travellers. Have you really both decided to go back to your own world?'

'Yes,' Cally said.

'Yes,' said Westerly. He reached his other hand across and gently touched her cheek.

'I am glad,' Lugan said. 'The islands are there forever, waiting for you, but life within time comes only once, and not again.'

He stepped out on to the beach in the moonlight. Its cold glow took all colour from his golden hair and cloak; his hair seemed white, and they saw much more strongly now the likeness of Taranis in his face. He touched each of them briefly on the shoulder. 'Go well – until I see you again.'

He raised one arm, the cloak billowing down from it like the sail of a boat, and pointed at the rockface before him, and where there had been rock there was a door. The beam from the lighthouse swung towards them over the sea. glinted on a heavy metal handle. and was gone.

Westerly reached for the handle and opened the door wide. They could see nothing beyond it. He took a deep breath. and looked at Cally. 'Goodbye, Cal.'

She was laughing at him. 'Hallo, West.'

Together they walked through the door. without looking back.

The lighthouse beam swung round again, over the waves. over the sand and rocks, like a slow pulse steadily beating, like the long unending swell of the sea.

FROGGETT'S REVENGE

K. M. Peyton

Danny Froggett is persecuted for being small – until help arrives in the form of a huge, hilarious dog.

TOM TIDDLER'S GROUND

John Rowe Townsend

Vic and Brain are given an old rowing boat, which leads to the unravelling of a mystery and a happy ending.

SLADE

John Tully

Slade has a mission – to investigate life on Earth. When Eddie discovers the truth about Slade he gets a whole lot more than he bargained for.